P~oint~. O~f~. V~iew~.

A Personal Perspective of the Bible
Volume 3

C. P. CLARKE

The characters and events portrayed in this book are based on the accounts written down in the Bible and creative license has been used to expand on the stories retold.

Cover design by: The Smithy Creative
www.thesmithycreative.co.uk

Other titles by the author:

Life In Shadows
Stalking The Daylight
The Killing
Vicky Rivers
Furi'on
POV - Volume 1 & 2
A Question of Faith
Stories on a Wall

www.cpclarke-author.com

Foreword:

POV has been something my dad (C. P. Clarke) has been reading to me for years. He started reading them as bedtime stories when I was younger before they became the first POV book. But now he reads them to me for me to check how to improve them and to make them better for the final result. Listening to these there have been some stories that I have thought weren't suitable for this volume and have been left out, but I hope to be seeing the new and improved versions in the future.

Personally I wouldn't say all the stories are suitable for a younger audience, they're not kids stories as they feature a few scenes of gore and drugs.

I think POV Volume 3 is one of the best of its kind, with modern day versions of all sorts of stories like The Good Samaritan (Badlands) and The Prodigal Son (The Jealous Brother). He has also added some of the poems and sketches that I have seen him perform.

I noticed when dad was reading them to me that he had cleverly put them into the chronological order they are in the Bible.

Whilst listening to the stories I realised that you get to know the character better from this point of view than in the Bible because it adds their thoughts and feelings during the story.

At some point I hope to be seeing stories from the Bible that aren't as well-known from a different point of view.

JJ Clarke

Contents

PREFACE: 1

AN EXHAUSTING WEEK 4

PHARAOH AND HIS MEN...............................5

THE COMPLAINERS 6

BLUBBER..10

HILLTOP SHOWDOWN 18

WITCH OF ENDOR 26

PRISON FOOD 28

HABBAKUK'S COMPLAINT..............................31

JOHN'S CHRISTMAS NARRATIVE 32

SIMEON..34

THE SICK HOST..39

DRAWING WATER..41

FEEDING THE HUNGRY 47

THE CLEAN UP 49

BLACK SHEEP OF THE FAMILY 52

THE JEALOUS BROTHER 55

OUT OF THE DARKNESS...................................66

BADLANDS 72

BADLANDS 80

THUGS AT THE GATE 84

A FATAL ERROR IN JUDGEMENT...................90

GRIEF..101

THE MOCKER 103

THE GUARD'S REPORT 108

PENTECOST 109

CHURCH 111

Preface:

This volume has been a long time in coming. My pace for writing these stories has slowed only due to the endless list of other writing projects that I've undertaken over the last couple of years.

The stories in Volume 1 were mainly short retellings that I'd written over a long period. Whereas the stories in Volume 2 were fewer but longer in length and purposely written for the book. This third volume is different again in the sense that some of the stories are purposely written for this book, but others were written years ago (the oldest going back to 1991 when I first became a Christian) and I have adapted them slightly to include them here, and have taken some risks in adding them in. Some of the accounts told by characters were written as performance pieces which I myself have performed in church (check out my website www.cpclarke-author.com or my YouTube channel to view some of the videos). Where I've felt it necessary I've made a note of explanation with the appropriate pieces.

I have had the privilege over many years of being able to perform, produce and direct, much of my own work, both on stage and in front of the camera, but mostly to small crowds of mainly church congregations within the context of creative services or missions where the use of drama or poetry has helped in communicating part of the message that Jesus loves us.

Here in this volume I have included just a few of those pieces, mixing in poetry with drama. In many cases the full written out script or story isn't what makes it to the stage but is adapted or shortened, or tailored to a specific need.

I always find it challenging to perform my material and am rarely totally satisfied with my own performance. Like any actor I can be a bit of a perfectionist in wanting it just right and rehearse it a thousand times in my head only to find that it is a very different and daunting experience playing it in front of a live audience.

One of the most challenging roles I've played is that of Judas. This was hard, not just because of the length of the piece, but mostly due to the emotional turmoil I had to put into the character in order to portray a man about to commit suicide. Coupled with that was the fact that, like most of my stories, this was my interpretation of the character and events. There is always the worry that some people won't get your take on it or try to argue that it's not biblical. Whenever I write a piece I write it with the scripture in front of me so that I stay true to the story, and any embellishments on my part are where the Bible is silent on the character's motives and therefore not going against what the Bible tells us nor against the spirit of the message it's trying to teach us.

There are a couple of stories included in this volume which are contemporary retellings. These are parables Jesus told which, being parables, lend themselves to a modern telling and are not strictly speaking 'point of view' stories but which I felt were worthy of inclusion in this volume.

There are often stories I write that I think might make it into a collection like this but for whatever reason they don't make the cut. One such story I thought worthy of inclusion in this volume, but due to its graphic content decided against adding, was a version of The Prodigal Son called The Burning Bin. It was one of the earliest stories I'd written way back when I first became a Christian. If you would like to read it I have published it on my website: www.cpclarke-author.com/read-extracts/. I have replaced it here with a different version of the same story, which was the last story to be written for this volume and is based off a play I wrote back in 2001.

I am eager to write many more stories and I have a growing list I am inspired to tackle. The books of Samuel are high on my 'to do' list!

As for my number one fan, I am so pleased that he has written the introduction to this volume and given it his seal of approval! Thanks son!

C. P. CLARKE

AN EXHAUSTING WEEK
(Genesis 1)

"In the beginning God created the heavens
And the earth."
He flicked the switch of the great yellow bulb
And there divided the day.
He split the sea from the sea,
Land from the sky
And then in the blink of an eye
There was life.
Then there was man - and later followed death.

A pretty exhausting week for some
Let alone one.
The perfect job.
Deadline, overtime
No cheating, plagiarising, no corners to cut
All thy own works.
It's no wonder he took a day off.

PHARAOH AND HIS MEN - ON THE RUN
(Exodus 14:23-28)

Fearful at the waters high
Life within swimming by
At heights above, beside their heads
Whilst feet and wheels of crested chariots
Impress imprints in bed so dry.

So why, unfathomable as it seems,
Have the slaves gathered on mass
Been granted such access
As they rush the steep bank afar.
The old man's staff raised
As they race across, a disorganised mess?

Confess their sins they may have done
As the walls of water loosened some
And panic filled the men.
No genius need to figure out,
As the soldiers began to run,
That their escape route was about to be undone.

None made it out that weren't Israelite
Not even Pharaoh with all his might
Could swim the walls that came crashing down
Smashing spears, swords, and chariots.
The Egyptian gods had lost the fight
As the army fell, lost to sight
The Red Sea swimming with their dead debris.

THE COMPLAINERS

(Numbers 16)

Oh, when are we going to learn? There's been so much death. Once again we're in mourning. Once again our rebellion has led to bloodshed. When will we ever learn?

We grumble and complain, never satisfied. Then something happens to halt us in our tracks and we silence our mouths until discontent rises up amongst us once more, and we start the cycle yet again.

Why don't we learn?

We are never happy. We weren't happy before we left Egypt, always complaining about the conditions and the tyranny of our masters. Then we complained about the attempts to break us free from the slavery there. Then, once we were free, we complained about being led to our doom with the sea before us and the army behind us. Then, when we escaped that, we complained about the lack of food. Then, when God provided food, we complained about the amount and the lack of variety. Then we complained about the disorganisation of our nomadic traipsing across the land and the lack of authority. So law and order was imposed, but guess what, we still weren't happy, we still complained.

You've got to feel sorry for the guys at the top, no matter what they do it's never going to be good enough. Despite all the miraculous signs of God's presence since leaving Egypt we still blame Moses and Aaron for all our hardships. How quickly we have forgotten our slavery.

The scouts returned recently with such bad news of the Promised Land that none of us dare to cross to it. We are all set to die here in the desert having followed that old fool and his brother.

Two of the scouts, Caleb and Joshua, say we're wrong. They say that the land is plentiful and that with the Lord's help we can overcome the obstacles that stand in our way, but the people don't believe it. I don't believe it.

I heard the accounts of the other scouts who spoke of giants and armies that roam the land. We may as well have stayed in Egypt if that is what we're walking into. We're all going to die out here.

I've lost count already at how many have perished.

Stop complaining! I say to myself. But I can't help it. I just don't trust in what I'm told, and it's easier to listen to the grumblings of discontent and the faithless than it is to God's appointed leaders.

I scratch at my skin. Irritated by the burning on my arms I cast my mind back to Taberah, that place we named after the fire burned through the outskirts of the settlement after we complained to Moses about all our hardships. Oh how the fire had raged through the camp that day!

You would have thought we'd have learned that none of us are excused from the consequences of our moaning, especially after Moses' own sister was struck down with leprosy for talking against her brother. Miriam healed up nicely after being cast outside the camp for a week, but still, how many signs does God have to throw at us before we get the point to quit moaning about things he's so clearly directed.

In a way we've kind of taken all the miracles for granted. We've seen all the amazing things God has done and how he's answered our complaints, and in favourable ways we don't deserve, yet we conveniently forget about them and moan at Moses and Aaron as if it's all their fault. At the end of the day we all left Egypt together, having seen God's call on us through the miracles. We could at any point have refused to come. We forget that all the other nations don't have a God that reveals himself in such a way that the people can see his power and majesty right there in front of them on a daily basis.

Yet still we complain.

You'd have thought that when the council tried to overthrow Moses and Aaron that maybe they would have reflected on all that has happened in the past: the miracles, the answered prayer, the fire and plague that came down when others went down that route. But no, Korah, Dathan and Abiram had them all riled up. There were about 250 of them there yesterday ready to usurp power from God's appointed leader. They put out an open challenge and half of us were hoping they would win over, but it was just foolish thinking.

We stood there watching, hoping God would be with Korah and give him new guidance as to where we should go next now that the Promised Land was out of the question. We watched as they lit their censers and raised their complaint to God. We watched as Moses rebuked them and prophesied what was about to happen to them. We watched as Korah, Dathan, and Abiram and their whole families, their tents, and all their possessions were swallowed whole by the earth.

The ground just opened up beneath them so suddenly that they had no escape, no chance to step to the side or jump for freedom. The land beneath them just gave way.

As we stood in shock and fear, fire darted out from the ground and struck the 250 stood by the burning coals they burnt as an offering. The fire consumed them. Even today I can smell the burnt flesh in my nostrils. Though that smell is being overtaken by something else as the rotting of something much closer to hand over shadows it.

This morning we all, on mass, turned to the Tent of Meeting where Moses and Aaron were and complained once again. They had caused the deaths of prominent men, leaders of our community. So what if it was their own rebellion against God that had been the root of it, we still blamed Moses and Aaron.

I remember seeing Moses frantically giving Aaron instructions about taking his censer and burning coals amongst the people. I didn't get it then as he ran around the crowd; there are thousands upon thousands of us so it's hard to make out what is going on at times.

It was only when I started to see people in the crowd who had been complaining with me begin to blister, their skin bubbling and peeling with the rapid onset of disease, that I realised a plague was spreading amongst us. Only when I saw people drop down dead around me did I begin to think upon all that had gone before, the results of our complaining and how obnoxious we must seem in God's eyes. He has been so patient with us, yet each time we just spit in his face.

I think I get it now. We just needed to be content and trust in God's provision, being thankful for what we do have instead of complaining about what we don't have. It's a lesson I think I've learnt too late.

I can see Aaron off in the distance trying to intercede to stop the plague, but I'm already on my knees in pain, my skin burning fire as blisters pop on my skin. I can see the plague slowing where Aaron is standing, but I can't get to him. I can't stand to walk. I don't even have the strength to crawl through the dust in his direction.

I try to call out, but he's not looking at me; his attention is only on those closest to him. If only he would look to me and move faster. My throat is now beginning to clam up, swelling, choking me, ensuring my complaining days are cut short.

BLUBBER
(Judges 3)

I guess the best way of describing Eglon would be 'fat'. He is a glutton. He is far beyond obese. Sweat trickles out of the rolls of blubber around his waistline like waterfalls from a cliff, only these cliffs have no sharp peaks or edges, just ripples of curve upon curve so that the expanded flesh appears at bursting point before folding over to the next layer, which hides the shape of what would ordinarily be a torso with limbs protruding.

The arms and legs of Eglon are but heavy weights of sagging skin wobbling like jelly under the strain of movement, the effort of which produces yet more perspiration.

The legs themselves appear not to have moved for some time as they appear red and blotchy, purple, almost black in places, stretched out in a reclined position upon a supported mattress of reinforced frame that lays before the throne of a once nimble king.

How Eglon got to this size is anyone's guess. An abuse of power and an idleness of riches is most likely. He certainly has the wealth to command others to do his bidding, and still controls the strength of brutality to exact his will upon his servants.

When he first took power he was half the man he is now, quite literally. Back then he fought in his own campaigns and commanded the respect of his army and his subjects. Now he just sits back getting fat, demanding his tributes are brought before him from the comfort of his secure palace.

For eighteen long years we have suffered his rule. All these long years this king of Moab has stood over us, having secured an alliance with the Ammonites and Amelekites to subdue us Israelites. It is for the evil of our people, our insistence on ignoring our God that we have been subjected to this humiliation and subjugation at the hands of this ungodly glutton.

If our forefathers could see us now they would be appalled. They suffered so much and travelled so far to bring us to this new land, flowing with milk and honey, the land God had provided for us, only to throw it away and be forced to bow down to this tyrant. Our Lord God must surely be displeased with us.

I have sought the Lord regarding what I can do to reclaim God's honour and begin to redeem our people for His glory. I have prayed. I have fasted. I have sought counsel. What I believe God has put on my heart I have kept to myself. King Eglon has spies everywhere. He might not be able to travel about himself but word certainly has a way of reaching his ears.

I have been selected. Our people have been crying out to the Lord, asking him how we should be released from the burden of our foreign rulers. They have felt it right to send a contingency of representatives to Moab to honour the king with a tribute, to placate him, to pacify him. Some think it will buy us favour so that he will leave us be for the coming year, others think that God will damn the king in accepting our tribute, but I know there is another plan. The fact that they have selected me to be the one to lead the tribute just confirms in me what my Lord expects of me. Am I scared? You bet I am!

As you can imagine the tribute is quite sizeable so it needs a number of us to carry and escort it all the way to the king. We don't want to just pass it off to one of his representatives locally, he has to know it has come from us.

I know the route. I've studied it. I know the obstacles in our path and what needs to be said to obtain safe passage. We cross the Jordan River safely and without incident and turn south to trail along the border of the kingdom of Ammon. As we tread this line between our two lands we come across an Ammonite patrol. I greet them and explain that our train of goods is bound for Moab as a tribute to the king. They seem satisfied and state that they will guide us down to the Moab border check point and see that we reach there safely. Although there is an alliance between the various nations everyone knows that the slightest offence could spark a war, so it is in the interest of the patrols to ensure a peaceful convoy gets through unassailed.

At the check point King Eglon's soldiers meet us with distain, peering down their noses at us as they inspect our duty and rifle through every cart and bag. They check us for weapons, but none of us have been foolish enough to carry a sword at our side. They look us over, pulling open our cloaks to our left side, and seeing no swords hanging there they let us pass with an official armed guide and directions on how to get to the palace.

It takes us some time as we march along and I can feel my skin blistering and tearing beneath my clothes as my right leg is irritated by the abrasive chafing of what lays there hidden, but I put up with the pain, knowing it's worth the discomfort.

Eventually we reach the palace and the soldiers that had been guiding us announce us at the gate. We are ushered into a forecourt and once again we, and what we have brought, are inspected.

We are then ushered through into an inner court where, in an upper room, the king can be seen looking down upon us from a balcony. I look up with disappointment in my heart as I realise the king will not be stepping down to greet us personally.

I bow and explain that we are Hebrews from Israel and have brought a tribute to appease the king. I gesture with my left hand at what we have brought into the courtyard. He smiles and waves, a royal dismissive gesture of thanks, now go.

I shout up words of praise and admiration to King Eglon on behalf of our people, hoping that what I have to say will gain me a private audience with him, but once again I am greeted with the half-hearted gesture of gratitude and dismissal. Clearly the king isn't interested, and nothing I have to say is likely to turn his head enough to draw him down to the courtyard to speak with us directly.

Placing our tribute on the ground we are then shown to the door and to the exit of the palace grounds. The same guards that brought us through the land seem eager to rejoin their own unit as they begin to march us back with haste.

We make our way as far as Gilgal when finally I pluck up enough courage to whisper to one of the guards that I have a private message for the king. It was something I had been brooding over ever since we had left the presence of the palace. I had run scenario after scenario through my head as to how to get the king to leave his chamber, and then it had struck me that the king would never leave and that I would need to find a way of getting myself up to him.

I tell our entourage that I need to go back, that there is something else I needed to do. They try to question me on it but all I say is that it is something God is requiring of me. My words seem to carry an authority that they recognise. God is with me in the same way he had been with me when I was chosen for this appointment, and this was something the people of God accepted and acknowledged, even if they didn't fully understand it.

They agree to go on without me and one of the guards agrees to take me back to the palace. After all, what threat could I be? I had been there once already without incident and had already passed their security checks.

As we enter the inner courtyard I repeat what I had told the guard, "Tell the king that I have a secret message for him." The officer disappears through a doorway and I can see him speaking to one of the king's bodyguards. A few minutes later I am guided into the inner rooms which are lit with torches, the light of the day having now faded so that most of the palace is now in gloom.

The officer pulls open the left side of my cloak and I give a look as if to so say `what again, how many times do you have to search me?'. He reads my look with an apologetic one of his own which says, 'sorry, just doing my job'.

He guides me up the stairs and bangs on the big double doors of the king's chambers. A heavy gruff voice lazily bellows for us to enter and the guard explains that I am one of the Israelites that had brought the earlier tribute and that I have a message for the king.

Inside the room I can see that the king has moved himself away from the balcony I had seen him at earlier and he is now perched upon a reclined seat within a wide chamber where before him lays a table of rich fruits and meats and goblets of wine.

I tilt my head in a half gesture to the bodyguard as I say that my message for the king is secret and for his ears only. He takes a moment in thought and I can see the curiosity spinning in his mind before it wins him over and he dismisses the guard.

I turn with the guard as I watch him leave, unfastening my clothing to the right of my cloak as I wait for the door to be firmly shut behind me. I grip the handle of what I have crafted by my own hand, then turn with my left hand beneath my cloak as though I am about to produce some evidence of whatever secret I am about to betray to the king.

"What is your name?" the king slobbers through a mouthful of food, having not taken in the introduction of the guard. I can see the juice and saliva trickle from the corner of his mouth as he speaks, rolling off his lip and onto the multiple curves of chin where it eventually gets lost in between the sweaty layers.

"I am Ehud. I have a message from God for you," I say as I climb the steps slowly towards him.

The king tries to push himself up from his seat to greet me, eager to bend an ear to my whispered words as I approach. My heart is beating wildly and a nervous bead of

14

sweat is forming on my brow. He isn't even standing by the time I pull the double edged sword I had made from beneath my clothing and thrust it forward hard with my left hand.

The blade goes deep, sinking into the soft rotund flesh of the king's waist, severing his intestines so that his guts immediately begin to flop out from the wide gash the sword has torn open from both edges of where it has pierced.

The king's eyes are wide with shock, the food he was still chewing on caught in his mouth preventing any sound escaping. Heavily he falls back down. I let go of the handle, seeing that it has sunk deep into his belly so that my hand is almost swallowed by the rolls of bloody fat that try to collapse over what I had held. As he splashes back down, the contents of all that blubber fall out upon the table of food at his feet, and I know then that he is dead.

Panicked, I look around at the sealed door behind me and know I am trapped. I hadn't thought through an escape plan and now I realise I have little time to come up with one. I had been purely focused on completing the task God had set before me. Now it is over my mind is frantic.

There is only one doorway in and that is heavily guarded. I go to it and find a key in the lock, I turn it slowly and quietly, wondering how long it will be before the guards figure out something is wrong. I am counting on the fact that they won't be too keen to interrupt the king if he is getting important information from a foreign land. Chances are they will hold off behind the door for as long as possible, just waiting. I look around the room; there is only one way I can go.

Stepping out onto the balcony I can see a couple of guards and attendants busy below in the courtyard. They have no reason to look up as they go about their own business. I can also see a corridor stretching from this wing of the palace toward a service gate at the far wall. The torches of servants light the way as they load up supplies onto a cart. It is a strange time of day to be leaving the palace with supplies and I am sure they have a valid reason for it, but I take it as a sign of God's provision and guidance as I assess the climb down from the balcony onto the roof of the corridor. In the dark it is hard to see the notches of stone I will need as hand and foot holds. I climb over, knowing I have to move swiftly and quietly.

I pray to my God that I will not be seen, that I will not stumble and fall, and that I will make it out of the palace unharmed. My Lord answers my prayers.

I scuttle along the roof of the corridor, passing by the stone statues that decorate the palace courtyard, and drop down behind the cart as the attendants are preparing the horses to lead it off. I find a space between two barrels and some sacks and hide myself there, trying to make myself appear as small as possible so should someone peer in I would be missed. The cart begins to move and I hold my breath, listening as we pass the gate. There are no checks as we leave. There is no need for suspicion of anyone leaving the royal palace.

I travel in the back of the cart for some miles before finally judging myself to be far enough away to be caught by an initial search of the immediate area around the palace. There is no way they will suspect me of having gotten so far away so quickly, and they are likely to spend hours searching the palace itself, suspecting that I would still be in hiding there.

Dropping onto the dusty road in the dark, my drivers blissfully unaware of the passage they have provided me with, I then stare up at the stars to gain an idea of which direction I need to head off in.

Turning to cut across the land I pray to God once more that I won't encounter any hostile forces or predatory beasts. I have no provisions with me so I am trusting in the Lord to sustain me. As I set off I hear the horns in the distance. They don't stop. They are a panicked call to arms and I can picture the leaderless soldiers running about in confusion unsure of what to do at the discovery of their dead king.

Running as fast as I can I eventually make it to a farmland where there are horses stabled in a barn. Finding water also, I refresh myself before sneaking away and then ride like the wind for home.

I make it as far as Seirah in the hill country of Ephraim. As I rode through the day I shouted to all the Israelites I passed that King Eglon was dead. Stopping now at Seirah I turn and see that a crowd has followed me, inspired by my words. I see that the people of God are with me. No, not just with me, they are following me as a leader. They fetch me a horn. I blow it as a call to arms and quickly I see men darting off to spread the word. No longer are we going to be subjects to Moab. Now is the time for battle and for reclaiming our land.

HILLTOP SHOWDOWN
(1 Kings 18:16-46)

Now you've probably heard about this one, it's quite a famous story. Everyone one for miles around has been talking about this. No matter where you go someone will ask 'did you hear about what happened on the mountain?', and then they'll proceed to tell you all about what they've heard. Sometimes they get it right, when the story hasn't been distorted and diluted by the official account the royal household has tried to put out. Sometimes you'll hear a pretty good version close enough to what I'm about to tell you, which is the true version. How do I know this version is correct? Well, like so many others, I was actually there.

Even if you're not from the region, an out of towner, a foreigner, you're sure to have heard of King Ahab and his wife, our illustrious queen, Jezebel. Ahab was renowned for being a pretty corrupt and evil king, but paired up with the Sidonian princess they are intolerable together. Now I'm not going to make any comments as to who wears the trousers in that relationship, Ahab, I'm sure, can hold his own, and as everyone knows you don't want to get on her bad side, but... who am I kidding? Ahab is well and truly under the thumb! If she says jump, he asks how high? If she says worship my god, he asks which one? If she says build me a high place to worship, he says wait, let me tear something down to make room first. You get the picture, right? So when she says kill all the prophets of the Hebrew God, you can bet a stack load of them went into hiding pretty sharpish. In fact Obadiah, the palace administrator, hid a hundred of them in two caves so that they wouldn't get slaughtered. A brave move for a guy who'd been tasked by the king to hunt out all the prophets and hand them over.

You see Obadiah believed in the true God and was faithful to him, so when he bumped into Elijah (the big cheese so far as the prophets went, and someone who was fast becoming Jezebel's number one object of aggression after speaking out against the practices of the royal family and for predicting doom and gloom on the nation) Obadiah was faithful to passing on Elijah's message to the king.

So the way I heard it is that Obadiah took back Elijah's message and the king agreed to meet with the prophet and the conversation went roughly like this:

King Ahab - So where have you been hiding out the last few years whilst we suffer the drought?

Elijah - You ignore God, that's what you get. You brought the drought upon yourself.

King Ahab - What do you want you troublemaking fool?

Elijah - I'm no troublemaker, you and your father's family are the troublemakers. It's your fault there's a drought. You don't follow God anymore but follow all those false gods, those Baals you've set up the high places for. I challenge you to a showdown of power between your gods and mine up on Mount Carmel. You bring your crew, your four hundred and fifty prophets of Baal and the four hundred prophets of Asherah who eat the scraps from the queen's table and I'll rock up with my God. Invite whoever you want to witness it and we'll see who has the real power.

King Ahab - Deal. I'll send word throughout the nation and invite the whole world to watch you make a fool of yourself. Then everyone will bow down to me and you'll face the fate of all the other doomsayers of your so called god.

Then they spat in the palm of their hands and shook on it. Ok, maybe that bit's made up.

Now if you haven't pieced it together yet as to why Jezebel was so hacked off with God's prophets in the first place then let me quickly explain. These prophets were God's mouthpiece on earth, they spoke his words unto the people and to the king. They were always advising the king about returning to the ways of God but the king's heart wouldn't listen to them as he bowed more and more to the whims of his wife. Then one day Elijah, speaking on behalf of God, said there would be no more rain, and guess what, no rain fell from that moment on. That was a hard and thirsty time as I recall. You couldn't get a decent jug of water anywhere and most people stank pretty bad because the rivers we washed in had dried up and nothing was growing so we were going hungry. It was during this time that Jezebel decided to take it out on God's boys and shut them up for good.

So there we are on the appointed day, early in the morning on Mount Carmel. The place is heaving. Now don't be thinking because it's called a mountain that it's a peak; it's mostly a long, low lying mountain range where there's plenty of hidden caves and enough flat land up there to provide a platform and a viewing gallery for thousands. And there were thousands! People came out of the woodwork from all over the region, some because they were brow beaten into it by the royal prophets and their followers, others because they wanted to see God's prophet triumph over the king, and yet others rocked up purely out of curiosity. Now I fell into that latter category. I didn't live far, so figured why not? Other than tending the fields what else did I have to do for entertainment?

My first impression, once I'd pushed and shoved my way to a suitable vantage point where I could see the proceedings, was that Elijah was one crazy dude! I mean, there he is fronting out almost a thousand enemy prophets and their followers who would much rather tear out his eyes and his tongue than allow him to speak God's word to the people, but he is just stood there unflinching, studying the crowd as they amass around him.

Eventually he speaks, addressing the crowd under the clear windless sky.

"How long will you sit on the fence, hedging your bets as to which god to follow? If the Lord is God, follow him; but if Baal is God, follow him."

That kind of got my attention. Not that I had an answer to it, but I, like so many others, had never heard the challenge so forcefully or with such authority. He was right. With the exception of the prophets, most of us were too weak in our faith to stand firm in our beliefs, and we were easily swayed and persuaded by those who pushed a different view of life.

In response to our collective silence Elijah responded.

"I am the only one of the Lord's prophets left [he didn't rile the crowd by accusing anyone as to what had happened to the rest, but we all knew the story] but Baal has four hundred and fifty prophets. Get two bulls for us. Let Baal's prophets choose one for themselves, and let them cut it into pieces and put it on the wood but not set fire to it. I will prepare the other bull and put it on the wood but not set fire to it. Then you call on the name of your god, and I will call on the name of the Lord. The god who answers by fire wins - he is God."

As I said, crazy dude!

No one complained at his suggestion. I guess everyone thought as I did, that no matter what he said, one man and his invisible god against the might of hundreds, with their carved idols of their gods and the weight of the king behind them, he didn't stand a chance; when this was over, Elijah was most likely a dead man.

There was plenty of dry wood lying about and it was quickly piled into two heaps. The prophets, I'm guessing figuring a sacrifice was on the cards, or maybe they just came prepared for any and every eventuality, had cattle on hand and at the ready. Between them they quickly separated their favourites and selected one for themselves and one for Elijah. It was no surprise that theirs was a fine, near perfect specimen for which please their god. Elijah's on the other hand was small and scrawny, and a pitiful offering.

The make-do sacrificial tables were built high as the crowd all pitched in with the scavenged donations to the cause. I busted a branch off of a dead tree, it snapped easily enough, having received nothing from the sky to nurture its decaying roots. I passed it forward, intrigued as to how this was going to play out. Part of me wanted the crazy fool to succeed just so that for once the underdog could win - everyone loves the underdog, right?

In good sporting spirit Elijah let the opposition go first. He instructed them to prepare their sacrifice but not to set the wood alight. The prophets of Baal slaughtered their bull and carved it up and placed the fresh meat upon the pyre ready to be burnt as an offering to their god. Then they prostrated themselves and called down on their god, calling on him to set the wood alight. The expectant minutes turned to hours and the desperate prayers, shouts and cries of the prophets went unheard by anyone in the heavenly realms. Quite a few of the crowd lost interest and drifted off. Some went away, down to the towns, and then came back again, me included. As the hours went by the whole thing got very boring. I love a good bit of conflict, watching two parties going at it in healthy competition, but this was just embarrassing. Watching these supposed holy men dancing around a dead bull and yelling for Baal to burn it up was seriously cringe worthy. Even Elijah was mocking them. "Shout louder!" he said. "Surely he is a god! Perhaps he is deep in thought, or busy dealing with something else on the other side of the world, or maybe he is taking a break or has gone on holiday. Maybe he is just taking a nap and can't hear you. Shout louder and wake him up!"

And so they did. And getting no answer they began to slash themselves with swords and spears as part of their ritual, and soon there was more blood from the prophets than there was from the bull. Frantically they called down upon their god from morning through to evening, yet still their call went unanswered.

Now whilst all this was going on Elijah had instructed for some of the wood to be carried over to the old altar of the Lord which had been torn down by Jezebel's zealots. He took twelve of the fallen blocks of the table and had the people stack them up to make a platform, exclaiming that they were to represent the twelve tribes of Israel. He had the wood placed on top of and around the repaired altar and then dug a trench around it. He then slaughtered the bull and cut it up and placed it on the wood for the sacrifice.

All the while the prophets of Baal were desperately pleading with their god to not be outdone by Elijah whom they kept glancing over at as he prepared to call down on his Lord.

Then the clown did the most curious thing. I call him a clown because this was just the most ludicrous thing I've ever seen and it made us all laugh to watch him do it. I wish I could have captured the look on the faces of some of the crowd when the jars were unveiled.

Elijah had clearly thought this through, having picked the location carefully and brought the things he needed. There were big heavy jars of water that he must have brought up the mountain with the help of others earlier. Like I said, it hadn't rained for a while so water was in short supply, yet he had managed to store up enough to waste on pouring all over his wood pile. He poured it into the trench and made sure the whole sacrificial heap was soaked.

The old fool then stood back and instructed for more jars to be filled and poured out on the wood.

Not satisfied that it was wet enough he told the people a third time to drench the table.

Even the prophets of Baal were laughing at this. It certainly distracted from their craziness and made their antics of the last few hours almost seem sane.

A few people called out with jibes of: 'How you going to light that when it's wet?'; 'Should have done that at lunchtime when the sun was stronger to dry it up!' 'I don't think your god is going to appreciate you making it difficult!'

Of course Elijah now had the ultimate excuse for his pyre not lighting; the wood was damp, but stupidly he'd wet it in front of the whole crowd. If he wanted an excuse for his god not performing he should have soaked it out of sight instead of making such a demonstration of the fact.

Of course, if you've all heard the stories then you know what happened next. I for one wasn't expecting it. Call me shortsighted. Call me dumb. Call me faithless. I was all those things, but not anymore. Lots of us changed our views that day. Lots of us aligned ourselves with the true God when we saw what happened next.

Elijah stepped forward, closed his eyes and in a loud voice spoke, not to the crowd but to God. "Lord, the God of Abraham, Isaac and Israel, let this lot see you today for what you are. Let them see that you are the true God and that what I've done here was all at your command. Show them Lord, so that they will turn their hearts back to you again."

That was pretty much all he said before a flame from Heaven lit up the whole scene. I say a flame from Heaven but to be honest I don't know where it came from, so sudden was its appearance that we were all pretty much blinded by it. The heat was immense, and those close by backed away before the flames licked out and caught them. The entire carcass was consumed, engulfed by the fire. Not just the sacrificial bull, but the wood and the water so that the ground around it where the trench had been dug was scorched dry. The only things still intact were the twelve stones of the altar.

I dropped to my knees immediately, as did most who were stood around watching. The whole mountaintop was filled with a holy reverence and fear.

When the crackling of the fire died down amidst the stunned silence, the prophets of Baal and Asherah stood awkwardly, a spectacle of embarrassment, to themselves and to the people.

Seeing them stood there we all began to call out and we bowed prostrate toward the altar. "The Lord - he is God! The Lord - he is God!" we cried aloud.

The prophets of Baal tried to shuffle away from the front of the crowd but Elijah saw them and commanded the people. "Seize them. Don't let any of them get away!"

They ran. We ran after them. That's the only time I've ever had to tackle a holy man. I threw myself at the heels of one of them and dragged him to the ground. When they had all been rounded up Elijah instructed that they be taken down to the Kishon Valley and slaughtered. There were plenty who were willing to carry out the command, but for me I didn't quite have the stomach for it. I handed over my prisoner, content that God's will was to be carried out by someone else.

Now in all this the king had hung back, observing but not really reacting or trying to interfere. In fact for most of it we had forgotten that King Ahab was even present. Now that this holy battle was won Elijah turned to the king and told him to go and get some supper because there was about to be a heavy downpour and if he hung about he would get caught in it. Ahab wasted no time in heading back to his palace.

I took the hint too and headed for the path down and for shelter. Others who didn't live nearby lingered to hide out in the caves. By the time I made it home I could see the first signs of clouds rising from the sea in the distance, and that night there was an almighty downpour that almost flooded the whole valley.

Now that's the truth of it, so if you hear any other versions that don't quite match up, remember, I was there.

WITCH OF ENDOR

(1 Samuel 28)

They come in, they pull open the tent
To hold my gypsy hand at my pagan table
My temple of death,
My curtain of deceit;
Here come custom, foolish fresh meat,
Hooded, ashamed, a need to be discreet
I care not his cause as I offer a seat.

"You know this is wrong, illegal, and of personal cost?"
I protest
Placing the guilt responsibility clearly on his chest.
He concedes and confirms the onus is his
As he brings forth the name of the one that is missed.

From the dead raise the prophet, I'll gladly deceive
And blind him with nonsense for the payment received.
Closed eyes, in trance, firm grip and a shake,
Conjure up Samuel I will...
for Saul's sake!
You're the king!
He's the prophet!
You'll have me killed
Slaughtered to join all else you've had snuff it.

You'll spare me you say, fine, but what about him?
He's real, not a fraud, a genuine apparition
An old man in robes rising disgruntled from the ground
Majesty, addressing you he be, such an unearthly sound;
The crown fallen prostrate with his request of political
unrest.

26

The dead it speaks in prophesy:
Tomorrows end of the monarchy
To battle defeated
To the grave the royal line.
Collapsed in dread went he.

"Wake up my king, wake up!
I did as you request, spare me please,
I'll feed you, send you on your way,
Not speak a word of this disgrace,
Not reveal your name or face,
Nor seek the dead.
A fearful lesson learned in this old witch's head.

PRISON FOOD
(Daniel 1: 1-21)

From my conversations thus far with these new foreigners that have been placed in my charge, it would seem there is plenty they are not happy with. Having been exiled from their homeland they now live here in Babylon, and although I can sympathise with their plight, I do not understand their grumblings about other things; they have after all been exalted above the rest and are living in relative luxury.

With their king gone and their treasures now stored in the temple of our god, these Israelites are now subjects of the king of Babylon. So they don't like the new names we've given them; ours role much nicer off the tongue. So they sneer at the restrictions placed upon their movements; they are still captives. So they don't want to give up their own religious practices; they are not in Jerusalem now and we do not bow down to their god.

These young men are fit and well. Not a blemish on their skin. Not an imperfection on their limbs; all fingers and toes accounted for. They are some of the finest looking young men of their race, even the heads of our own women have turned in their direction. They will be, once they have finished their training, quite an asset at the king's table.

Three years I must spend educating them in our language and ways. Three years I have to mould them into upstanding citizens acceptable before the king. Three years to make them more loyal to our nation than they are to their people and their god. It is a challenge that is harder than it sounds.

These young men are stubborn hearted and bold in their resistance of the changes I wish to make. In truth I care little what they think privately so long as the results of my labour are reflected before the king. If they should embarrass me or show me a failure in any way then it will be I who must answer for it. There are devastating penalties for those who displease the king; a striking with the sword would be a merciful death compared to the lion's den or the fiery furnace.

I converse with the young men in my charge on a daily basis in the lecture hall prescribed for such occasions. There are a great number of them but I suspect most won't last the distance. They will displease me, or the king, in some way: rebelling, arguing, failing in their tasks and studies. Of the group there are four who stand out above the rest, they are the ones from Judah: Daniel, whom I have given the name Belteshazzar; Hananiah, who is now called Shadrach; Mishael, who is now Meshach, and lastly Azariah, whom I have named Abednego. Of these I have taken a keen interest and liking to Belteshazzar. I see a bright and illustrious future ahead of him, if he lasts the course. His only downside is his persistence in giving honour to his god.

These selected Israelites are provided with food from the kings table: choice cuts of meat, garnished with such delicacies that have been gathered from the four corners of the world we occupy, fresh fruit and vegetables, all with copious amounts of the finest wine to wash it down with. You would think that with all this there would be no grumbling about the diet, but no, Belteshazzar is not happy.

Were it anyone else I would have dismissed his objections out of hand, but the young man is a keen negotiator and knows how to present an argument well. As I said, the king would be pleased with him. Belteshazzar, though, finds the food not to his pleasing. He says that it is unclean and that he is defiling himself before his god by accepting it into his body. To be honest I don't quite understand it. Their whole religion seems set upon rules of tradition that are layered with multiple ways to displease their god. I find it hard to keep up with and so have stopped trying to make sense of it. It must be just as hard for them to understand our ways and practices. For this reason I am willing to give Belteshazzar some slack and entertain his arguments.

Ten days he says. He wants me to let him and his three friends eat only vegetables and drink only water for ten days. I explained that if they come over sick, or lose weight, or become faint and pale in the skin, and it becomes known that they haven't been receiving their allotted food then it would be my head that would be on the block, quite literally. Belteshazzar acknowledged my objection but said that after ten days if they looked any less for wear than the others then they would resume eating the same as the rest, but if they looked just as healthy then he requested I serve them only the vegetables in the future.

I shook my head quite adamantly. There was no way I could bow to such a request, not publically, not directly.

I knew Belteshazzar had made the same request of the guard who brought their food. Whether he approached him before he approached me I wasn't sure, but the guard had enough sense to confide in me. I gave him a non-committal response, basically saying that I didn't condone it but should he choose to accept the young man's challenge then the results would be at his own risk.

It has been far longer than the ten days Belteshazzar requested and I honestly don't know what food the guard has been giving them; I don't dare enquire as I judge it better that I don't know. What I can say is that all four of the young men look just as strong and vibrant as the others. Their minds are just as quick, if not quicker, and they seem to have a joy about them which makes me think they are not saddened at displeasing their god.

If it is true that they are restricting their food by imposing their own religious diet, then it would appear that their god is feeding them with something that provides far more sustenance than the table of our king can provide.

HABBAKUK'S COMPLAINT
(Habbakuk 1:2-4)

How long, Lord, must I keep banging my head against this
brick wall?
My head is sore and bleeding from the endless
complaining,
But, it seems, it's all falling on deaf ears.
Can't you hear me?
I've been yelling out about the endless violence,
It's all around,
Yet you don't save the victims.
I'm forced to witness the injustice of so many,
It's all around,
Yet you seem to put up with it,
I don't understand why?
There's grief all around,
The papers and TV are full of it:
Destruction and violence
Conflict and strife,
And that's putting it mildly.
The police are powerless
And the courts are a joke.
The criminals and thugs outnumber those good
Law abiding citizens,
So that they always win by playing the system
And we, as always, are penalised.

JOHN'S CHRISTMAS NARRATIVE

This was originally a drama piece to fit in with a creative Christmas service based on John 1 and expanding on the parts of the story missing from his Gospel. I have removed all the stage direction and tidied up the monologue for this version.

CPC

The story I'm about to tell you may have heard before. By now the word has spread far and wide. This account was told to me, John, by my friend Jesus and those others with whom he travelled. You see, in the beginning was the Word, and the Word was with God, and the Word was God. He was with God in the beginning.

Let me tell you how the Word became flesh.

I only knew Mary as an old woman, she became like a mother to me, but when she was a young girl, in the days when she was engaged to be married to Joseph, an angel of the Lord appeared to her and told her that she would bare God's son, even though she was still a virgin.

Joseph was later instructed by the angel to name the boy Jesus, and so he did. I imagine it must have been hard for Joseph, facing the challenge of raising a son that wasn't his own, who was perfect in every way, and who knew your every fault. Jesus, as I knew him as a man, could look right into your soul, there was no one else like him.

Anyway back to the story. Forgive my rambling, there is just so much I could tell you about my friend Jesus. There was a census, and everyone had to go to their home towns. Now Joseph was a descendant of King David, so he took the, by this time, very pregnant Mary, to Bethlehem, the town of David, but the Inn was full. No one had a room for them. Eventually someone let them use their animal stable. And there, amongst the dirt and filth and the noise of the animals, Jesus, our great Lord and Saviour was born.

Now I've heard and seen many miraculous things since getting to know Jesus as a friend so I don't doubt anything about what I've been told about his birth. Apparently, not long after he was born, shepherds came and found them at the stables saying that a chorus of angels had appeared to them proclaiming the birth of the Messiah, the Christ. Not only that but there had been a bizarre bright star tracing the sky which rested over Bethlehem, and three eastern rich men, nobles or kings or something, turned up with gifts for Jesus, this baby they'd never seen before. Surely not the birth of any ordinary man.

There's a lot more to Jesus' story. There really is too much to tell in one go, but I've written some of it down, in case you want to read it. Others I know have written more detail about what I've said about Jesus' birth, so I'm sure you'll get to hear more about it one way or another.

SIMEON
(Luke 2:25-35)

I can't tell you how old I am, except to say that I have lived longer than I should have. What has prolonged my life is a promise from God that I would see the messiah before I died.

Have you heard of the signs recently? The strange star in the sky, and the wild tales told by the shepherds of angelic beings singing on the hilltops. In themselves they maybe nothing, but together, with the expectancy of a saviour from God, they speak of something wonderful: a child born to us like no other.

I have been coming to the temple courts regularly looking out for the promised one. I have looked into the eyes of many a man and child over the years, but none have reflected back the glory of God I am keen to recognise.

Here I stand again, in this temple, waiting. I study the crowd, the faces passing by as they enter, and those sat in prayer, looking expectantly. There is a couple who have entered; she carries a child, a new born baby. The shepherds, they spoke of a baby. I must see this child.

The father carries the animal sacrifices for the purification of the child, to dedicate him to God. Excuse me, make way, I must get near, I must see this child.

Hello, my name is Simeon, may I look at your child. Thank you. A boy. His eyes - there is no doubt. At last I have seen. Sovereign Lord, now let your servant die in peace, as you have promised. I have seen your salvation, which you have prepared for all people. He is a light to reveal God to the nations, and he is the glory of your people Israel!

His mother seems pleased as I bless her family and tell her of the greatness of her son.

I am ready to depart this life knowing that there is a light to shine the way ahead for the world I leave behind.

CALLED OUT
(Matthew 2:13-23)

So there we were hiding out, waiting. We didn't know how long it would take but we were confident that this was the right course of action. I had told my wife what the messenger had said. She believed me, trusted in me, and we both trusted our source as we left our old life behind based on the information we received.

It had been a few years and we had no idea what was happening back home. We heard snippets of news from traders and other travellers whom we came across occasionally that had journeyed to Egypt from Judea, but word was scarce and we didn't want to draw attention to ourselves by asking too many questions.

Our family was growing but we were far from settled, in our hearts at least, and none there knew the scandal that had beset our marriage at the outset, nor the wonder that begun our parenting, nor the horror that caused us to flee.

We, of course, had heard about the massacre as we travelled west, having packed up our things quickly during the night and hit the road to evade what was coming. We had been tipped off about the soldiers by our source, he who had already proven to be so reliable. It was he again that came to me last night with fresh news and instruction.

I don't know how many toddlers there were in the town we left behind, not many, it being relatively small, but the number didn't diminish the horror of what happened. The king was well known for his barbaric brutality over the forty years he had reigned as king over Judea. He was known to have killed many who opposed him or whom he didn't trust, his family were no exception, having executed his wife, three of his sons, his mother-in-law and countless others. Now he could add the slaughter of innocent children to his fame, all thanks to his jealousy and fear that the prophesy would be fulfilled that would see the Jews delivered from its foreign rulers by a Messiah.

It was our son the king was after. Not that on appearance our eldest is anything special to look at. He is a normal child, strong and healthy, cheeky and playful.

We know the scriptures well, and have studied them even more since we became aware of the special value of the child we brought into this world. I, being of Davidic heritage, and my son being born in Bethlehem, fulfilled part of an age old prophesy about the Messiah, God's great saviour our people are expecting. It was a prophesy King Herod feared would happen in the generation of his sons. Yet that alone was not enough to set the soldiers upon us. What upset Herod the Great was the homage shown the boy by the Magi, the wise men who came from far away in the east.

The Magi brought our son gifts, things of value that would only be bestowed on a king. We were amazed and thankful as we accepted the gifts on behalf of the boy. They told us they had followed a star that foretold of a royal birth. They also told of how Herod had intercepted the travelling train of wise men before they had reached us, and innocently they had told the king where they were heading as they sought guidance and permission and safe passage to travel through the land. It was this news that would have unsettled Herod as he was already in constant fear of his throne being usurped from under him.

When the wise men didn't return to tell the king that they had found the child and whose home he could be found in, the king was furious and sent his soldiers to kill every child in the town that looked to have been born within the few years the Magi had indicated.

We escaped just in time. The gift of gold from the wise men affording us passage and provision of a home as we fled to this foreign land.

It was a lot to risk for a child that is not my own. He is mine in every sense, except that I am not his natural father. Word of who the father was came to me the first time I

36

encountered my secret messenger, the one whose timely interventions have proved so pivotal in the passage of our journey as a family. It was he that encouraged me to stay with Mary, even though I doubted her honour when I discovered her pregnancy before our marriage. It was he that confirmed to me that Mary was honourable and true a wife as could be. It was he that told me the unborn child was conceived of God himself. Crazy as it sounds I accepted it as truth, and the evidence of his birth confirmed it.

There are such stories to tell from when Jesus was born. Strange movements in the skies, shepherds visiting telling of angelic hosts proclaiming a king born to us, and then of course the Magi who came sometime later.

They had a vision too, a dream, a message telling them to avoid Herod's path on their return journey home. I have always wondered whether the one that delivered their message was the same as the one that delivers mine. Run, flee, he had said. By now I knew enough to trust that voice that spoke God's words of kindness, guidance, and protection so clearly in my dreams.

That same voice came to me there in that foreign land. Call him an angel, a messenger from God, a friend. His word is always true. He told me that our days of living in exile were at an end, that it was time to return home to Israel, that Herod the Great was dead.

So that very day we began to make our plans to return home, packing up our things and selling what belongings we couldn't travel with. We gathered as a family to go home to the land of our people, the Jews, to whom Jesus has been called as saviour, as Messiah.

I, as his father, have vowed to keep him safe until he is old enough to fulfil his role. I don't know what it all means for him or our people, but I do know I must take him to where he belongs, to where he is called. Whatever the future holds for us as a family and for my son Jesus, it is not in Egypt but in the land of our forefathers.

Admittedly I was cautious as we returned to Israel, passing through Philistia to Judea. I got word that Archelaus was now king, not that his morals are any better than that of his late father. I reasoned that there would be a chance he would be ignorant of who we were and the unreasonable fear and jealousy of his father that had caused us to flee in the first place. I was also hoping his mind would be more fixed on cementing his new rule and appeasing those foreign rulers that had put him in power. Despite this though, I was fearful. I kept picturing the slaughtered children we had left behind in Bethlehem and I had more than just one child to keep safe now.

There has been whisper amongst the traders of late of unrest in Judea; already it would seem the people are not happy with their new king.

That same voice came to me last night in a dream not to linger in Judea and not to stop at Bethlehem, but to move north to Galilee. Archelaus' brother Antipas now rules that region. I don't know what lies ahead on this road we tread, but I will trust my guide once again.

THE SICK HOST

(Luke 4:38-41)

I'm dizzy. I'm nauseous. My skin is clammy yet I'm burning up, with sweat soaking my bed clothes. I should be in the front room seeing to my guests, not hidden away back here coughing and spluttering as though I were on my death bed.

Silly old woman! I must muster the strength to get up.

I swing my legs forward and push myself up, but all too quickly I'm down again, almost collapsing painfully to the hard mat. I groan loudly in pain and discomfort. I try to stifle it but it's too late. I can hear my son-in-law's footsteps of concern as he tears himself away from his friends.

They're a good bunch that he hangs with these days. Not that he used to hang with a bad crowd before, but these guys seem to have a bond, a common purpose. Mostly his friends were all fisherman in the past, but now there is a collection of different, new, friends. Both Simon and his brother Andrew are still quite close with Zebedee's boys, James and John, they've known each other since they were kids, but now they and the others follow this new teacher around. They hang on his every word and go wherever he goes.

I shake my head as I feel the heaviness trying to force me back down to the mat. My place is serving my guests. This is my home. My daughter is in there holding the fort but that's not quite the same, especially as this teacher has deemed it fit to preach from my living room.

A shadow appears at the door and I can see through my clouded vision the silhouette of my son-in-law. He draws close, crouches down and feels my brow.

"Mother, you are burning up, let me get the teacher, he can help."

39

I am too weak to protest. I smile wanly and try to rest my head back down as I watch Simon shuffle back out to the other room.

A few minutes pass, or a few seconds, I can't tell; time is moving slowly as I try not to throw up. Simon comes back leading Jesus into the room. Suddenly I'm worried about my appearance. How do I look? Is my hair ok? Oh my word I'm not even dressed! I wonder whether the shock of my predicament shows on my face. I want to apologise. I want to tell him not to trouble himself over me. I want to tell him I will be okay and will come out and serve him a meal shortly.

He bends down to me. I see his beard ruffle as his cheeks upturn. He lays a hand on my forehead and the other on my shoulder, then looks up to the roof muttering something I can't make out. Then he stands and back steps to the door urging my son to leave me to get dressed.

As soon as they are out of the room I feel so much better. My head is no longer pounding and my throat is no longer choked with the closeness of fever. I sit up and breathe deeply. My aching joints of moments ago don't hold me back as my eyes scour the room for something suitable to wear. There is a bowl of water on the floor by the bed which my daughter had been using to keep me cool earlier. I dip my hands in and splash my face, smiling, feeling better than I've felt in a long time. I feel like ten years have been lifted from my aging frame.

I can hear the chatter in the other room clearly now, no longer dulled. It would seem I have quite a houseful and I am eager to meet their needs. I'm sure once they see what the teacher has done for me we'll be swamped with more guests wanting a touch of the same treatment, and really, who could blame them!

DRAWING WATER
(John 4:1-42)

It was a hot day, I remember it well. I'd gone to the well about noon to draw water. A few of the other girls would usually go at this time, generally those like me who didn't want to be seen by a crowd. Midday was the quiet period as most people were smart enough to draw water at either end of the day when it was cooler. I avoided the busy rush hours. I didn't like the crowds. I didn't care for the scowling faces and sideways snipes of aloof judgement. I didn't care for the condescending comments and sneers and the way they all seemed to look down their noses at me.

There was a Jew sat by the well when I arrived with my jars. He looked pretty ordinary and unassuming as he sat there taking in the view of the land. I assumed he was waiting for someone, as often people would use the landmark of the well as a meeting point. I skirted around him, keeping my head low and trying not to make eye contact, stepping to the opposite side of the well to avoid him.

I tied my jug to the rope and lowered it quickly, keeping my eyes staring down into the darkness below. I could feel the Jew staring at me and for once I wished one of the other younger girls was there to distract the attention off me.

Carefully I raised the jar from the deep pit it had dropped to, eager to be away heading back to town. The sound of the water slopped back up at me from the darkness below as I pulled hard on the rope. As my jar swung up, water dripping off it to fall back down the hole, I lifted it off to place on the ground and readied myself to lower another. Just then the man spoke. "Will you give me a drink?" he asked.

I was taken aback by the request. He was a Jew. I was a Samaritan. Surely he knew that. Surely he knew that asking me for water would make him unclean; these Jews saw all us Samaritans as detestable and misguided. I pointed out the fact that this would not be proper, more for his sake than for mine. I didn't know him and didn't want to encourage any impropriety, or for him to think that simply because we were alone that I would act inappropriately. I may have a reputation but that doesn't mean I'll turn my head for any and every man.

This was Sychar in Samaria. He could not have been mistaken as to me being a Samaritan.

He spoke again. My eyes were still lowered avoiding his gaze as I kept my distance.

"If you knew the gift of God and who it is that asks you for a drink, you would have asked him and he would have given you living water."

What he said made no sense to me. I stood confused for a moment trying to work out what he was trying to say. Gifts from God and living water had me stumped. I had no idea what he was talking about, but he seemed to be implying that he was a Jew of some importance. Maybe he was famous where he came from, but I didn't have a clue who he was. If offering me a drink was some sort of chat up line then he was going to be sorely disappointed. I certainly wasn't going to accept a drink from him if he drew it from the well for me, that would be totally improper.

I tipped my head up and noted that he had nothing with him with which to draw water, and the water was too low down for him to reach in. Seeing this I relaxed a little and pondered further this living water he spoke of. If he knew where he was, which I assumed he did, even people from out of town knew that this was Jacob's well, which Jacob himself had given to us and had used for his family and animals, then what was he claiming? Did he think he was greater than Jacob and could provide water fresher than that which our well gave up? I made my thoughts loud, trying

42

to tame the scoffing tone in my voice as I reacted to his pretentious superiority over me.

The man responded with a gentle tone in contrast to the air of distain that had expelled from my mouth, and what he said was intriguing and, dare I say it, attractive.

"Everyone who drinks this water will be thirsty again, but whoever drinks the water I give him will never thirst. Indeed, the water I give him will become to him a spring of water welling up to eternal life."

I raised my eyes to look at him. He didn't look away as I had hoped; he met my challenge with a piercing gaze that was captivating. I don't know whether it was his eyes searching my soul or the words that he spoke, but something deep within me lit up in a way that I just couldn't quite explain. Suddenly I was eager for this living water he spoke of. A drink that would satisfy. I'd never had anything which had fully satisfied me and I lived with a constant whole in my heart waiting to be filled. Maybe that was why I tried to fill my life with the comfort of a man as I never felt totally complete on my own.

"Give me this living water so that I don't have to keep coming back here looking to be refreshed," I begged, daring to step around the well to get closer to him.

"Go, call your husband and come back."

At his words I stopped in my tracks and sunk both my head and shoulders. I didn't want to go back to get the man in my life. He was the reason I avoided the crowds. He was the reason the people looked down on me. Well, not him specifically, but my track record in the community left me unworthy. This living water was to be bestowed on my husband, and I could receive it through him. Suddenly I realised that what was being offered I would be excluded from.

Downcast, staring at the dust on my feet I said, "I have no husband."

"You are right when you say you have no husband," he said, and as he spoke I knew he was condemning me, seeing through me and speaking God's judgement upon me as one of his prophets. "The fact is, you have had five husbands, and the man you now have is not your husband. What you have said is quite true."

My mouth dropped open in awe. There was no way he could know that unless God had told him. I had never seen him before. He had never met me. We were strangers to each other. Yet somehow this man knew all the things that had happened in my life and I knew there was no hiding anything from him. He knew me intimately without me ever having said a word about the life I'd lived.

My mind span. Guilt and shame flushing my face with embarrassment. I wanted desperately to change the course of the conversation. I didn't want my life laid bare in front of this prophet. I didn't want all my sin and shame dredged up and spread out on the ground before me. His people, the Jews, always disputed with us Samaritans where we should worship and it was a great cause of hostility between us. We worshiped on the mountain and they worshiped in Jerusalem. I thought if I could sway the conversation to that argument it would deflect his attention from the rot in my life.

I rattled off my dispute quickly, to which he replied, "Believe me, woman, a time is coming when you will worship the Father neither on this mountain nor in Jerusalem. You Samaritans worship what you do not know; we worship what we do know, for salvation is from the Jews. Yet a time is coming and has now come when the true worshipers will worship the Father in spirit and truth, for they are the kind of worshipers the Father seeks. God is spirit, and his worshipers must worship in spirit and in truth."

I could have screamed my frustration then. I had come to the well to draw water not attention to myself. The last thing I wanted was to get into a theological debate with some stranger. I tried thinking of a way out of the conversation and backing away from the well as my mind tripped over the words he'd spewed out at me. What he said played very much on the differences between what our two peoples believed and I had to admit that I was ignorant of much of what the Jews claimed to know about scripture. I didn't want to seem dumb before this stranger but there were gaps in my knowledge, so I piped up by saying that I knew a messiah was coming. "When he comes," I said, "he will explain everything to us."

My legs gave way with what he said next as I slumped to the edge of the well and sat down.

"I who speak to you am he," he said.

He was a prophet, I had ascertained as much already. I was undeniably and inexplicably drawn to him, despite of, or maybe because of, my desperate attempts to back away. I knew what I sensed was true and his claim to be the messiah just rocked my world. Why was the prophesied Messiah taking the time to talk with me, an outcast of society, a sinner who couldn't bear to face those in her own community, and a Samaritan at that? Why was he was taking the time to explain the mysteries of God to me? He had asked me, a woman, with all my failings and imperfections, for water. It wasn't something he had to do, no one was watching. He could have ignored me.

Just then a group of men strode up to the well and appeared behind me. The prophet had seen them coming and seemed unperturbed by their presence, clearly knowing who they were. There was surprise on the faces of the men that the prophet was talking with me, but none of them questioned him about it, nor held me in judgement as the man himself seemed to accept me, even in their presence.

As the men began to talk with their master I slipped away, not out of fear or shame as I had wanted to do earlier, as in the way I had approached the well. I had come with one outlook and left with another. I'd had an encounter with someone who could see right through me and knew my inner soul, and as a result I felt a change in my heart. I walked back to town as quickly as I could, having left my water jars behind. Gathering water from the well didn't seem that important anymore.

I found some friends in the town and urged them to come back to the well with me, telling them that I had met a man who told me everything I ever did and, though already knowing it in my heart, I asked them whether this man could possibly be the Messiah.

Rallied up by my excitement a crowd gathered behind me as I returned to the well. He and his companions were still there, and so we stood and listened to all the man had to say to us. I learned then that his name was Jesus, and many of the townspeople believed his words. They even invited him to stay in the town, and he and his friends did just that, teaching us about the ways of God for two days.

It's hard to think that before Jesus arrived in our town I felt little more than an outcast, a sinner looked down upon by my peers because of my past. Now those same people have said to me that they believe in Jesus, initially out of curiosity over what I had said about him, but now because they had heard him for themselves. He really is the Saviour of the world, they say to me excitedly, talking to me as an equal and no longer as someone with a soiled history and carrying dirty baggage.

FEEDING THE HUNGRY
(Matthew 14:13-21)

The people were hounding
Surrounding, demanding,
Persistent to the point
Pointless resisting.
On the heights they listened
As he spoke to their hearts
Their stomachs distracted by the lack of food carts.
Send them to eat he declared
As the day began to unwind.
And whine did his followers about food
Or lack of
And the hour of the day
And the money they'd have to spend
If for the whole crowd they'd have to pay.
But feed them he'd said.
What scraps can you find?
Five loaves of bread and two fish
Courtesy of this here young lad.
But even that was not enough
To the shrewdest calculating mind.

Five thousand men
Their wives and their kids
All hungry and waiting
Anticipating as they were shepherded into groups.
Fifties and hundreds all crammed together
As thanks was given up
As the scraps were passed around
And around
And the fill was too much.
Confusion, bewilderment
Where from came so much?
Twelve baskets left over
And none were left hungry
No stomach left empty as they all drifted away
Having all had enough.

THE CLEAN UP
(MARK 2: 1-12)

Enter a man with a broom sweeping the floor, he looks annoyed.

"Fanatics. Idiots. Careless... reckless... *[stops and sighs]*. And who gets to clear up the mess, eh! And I notice no one's mentioned who's going to pay for the damage.

I don't know, I mean you open up your home in good faith and look what happens. Don't get me wrong, I've got nothing against them holding their meetings here, I wouldn't have offered if I was against it would I, but please, a little respect.

Oh, what you didn't hear what they did. Oh well, let me tell you.

Everyone was buzzing 'cause Jesus was in town. Everyone's heard of what he can do, right? So everyone came here to hear what he had to say, and let's face it everyone wanted to see him perform a miracle. The place was packed. I tried stopping people from coming in but it was no good, there were too many of them; they smashed come of my best jars and ornaments. *[shakes his head]* There was that really nice one I got from the temple in Jerusalem last Passover.

Anyway, Jesus is babbling on, everyone's captivated, and I'm watching my gear carefully to make sure no one's helping themselves – if you know what I mean. Then all of a sudden there's this clamoring about outside, raised voices amongst the crowd. I couldn't get to the door so I couldn't see what was going on. It went on for a few minutes and then all of a sudden there's this thumping sound above. I ignored it at first. Heads started turning up. I didn't look; I guess I was trying to deny that it was happening. But the noise was getting too loud. When I did look up I could see the roof vibrating and dust falling from the ceiling. Then all of a sudden a hole appeared in my roof. Can you adam and eve it, these lunatics were tearing my roof open to get in to see Jesus! And then I realised that there was nothing I could do about it.

I was yelling at them to stop but that went unheard. Eventually there was a hushed silence as sunlight poured through the huge hole they'd made. I could see these four faces looking down, then they disappeared. A moment later this bloke is being lowered down on a stretcher.

It's funny how floor space suddenly appears when you think something's going to land on your head.

Everyone looked shocked. Everyone! Except for Jesus. You know he was smiling, and then he said to the guy on the stretcher, who appeared to be paralysed, "Son your sins are forgiven."

And that was it, it really kicked off then. What happened next kinda made it all worthwhile. The Pharisees got on their high horse about who could forgive sins. Jesus made some rebuke about what was easier, forgiving sins or healing the paralysed bloke on the stretcher. The exchange was priceless. *[looks up at his roof]* I should have charged an entrance fee, ticket prices would have gone through the roof. *[laughs wryly]*

Anyway, he does it don't he. This guy can really put on a show, and he's a real crowd pleaser too – unless you're a Pharisee of course. "Get up and pick up your mat," he says to the bloke. Which he does of course, to the stunned silence of everyone as he stands and walks out with this big grin on his face. Picture it, this crippled geezer walking calmly past this crowd paralysed by the shock and amazement of what Jesus had done.

Oh they all got moving eventually. *[continues sweeping]* Jesus and his mates were keen to get out after that, don't blame them really, it could have got quite tricky what with the way the Pharisees were reacting.

So here I am, clearing up the mess. I tell you if these things are going to keep happening I'm not sure I want to keep hosting the home group at my house."

BLACK SHEEP OF THE FAMILY
(Mark 3:20-35)

Now we all know Jesus is special, right? A right special case, if you know what I mean. We'd seen his tricks, his party pieces. He is quite the magician, but he's never disclosed his secrets and told us how he does it. Ever since he'd turned water into wine at the wedding he's had us guessing and trying to replicate these so called miracles. We've had our wild theories, but to be honest the latest set of healings have us stumped. We figured he's been paying others to help set them up somehow. Of course, being my older brother, mum would never let us badger him about it. Mostly she seems accepting of his bizarre behaviour.

It's got so bad that even some teachers of the law have come down from Jerusalem to check out what all the fuss is about. They'd heard that there was a man teaching the people about God and performing miracles. Naturally worried that this was some sort of deceiver trying to stir up trouble with the Romans, or trying to make a false claim to being the messiah everyone is expecting to free our people from our oppressive occupiers, they were compelled to come and quickly debunk it.

Word came to us via a friend in town who sought us out and said we needed to take charge of our brother who's been teaching in a house packed full of people. He was bringing shame upon us. Everyone knows we're related. He seems to care little for the impact his antics are having on the rest of the family. It reflects badly on us all. Everyone locally knows he's only a carpenter, born of a carpenter. As the eldest he is expected to look after our mother, but instead he is shirking his responsibilities and leaving it to us, his younger siblings.

Mother, as usual, doesn't overly complain. She only seems to care that he isn't doing too much, concerned only that he's not overdoing it and tiring himself out. He's always been her favourite. He's the one she always allows to do his own thing. She always seems to think he knows best. Just like the time he went missing for days when we were kids on that trip to Jerusalem. We were all going frantic thinking something bad had happened to him, but no, there he was sitting comfortably in the temple chewing the fat with the teachers of the law as though nothing was amiss. I don't think he even gave a thought to the rest of us. He gave his excuses about why he was there, and our folks just accepted it. Mum had always seemed to bow to his authority, even when our father had still been alive.

Of course we protest, nagging her to treat us equally and to stop taking his side over everything. We try to tell her how much of a mockery he is making of the family, and how people will start to treat her if she doesn't warn him sternly to calm his behaviour. If he has to keep running this scam he could at least do it far from home where no one knows us.

The house he's speaking in is ram packed with people trying to hear his teaching, but mostly they just want to see a miracle.

As we reach the door the teachers of the law whom have come down to check him out are outside exclaiming that Jesus is possessed by Beelzebub, calling him the Prince of Demons and saying that he is using dark arts to perform his miracles. Apparently they have heard and seen enough and have made up their minds, coming to the conclusion that he is dangerous. They are about to head back in to convince the crowd and challenge Jesus publically when we brothers and our mother rock up and stop them.

"Wait," I say, "we are his family, and I tell you he is not of his right mind. He's not evil, he's just gone a little crazy."

They look down on us and scoff at us before turning away to push through the crowd to assert their authority inside.

Our friend, the one who told us about the meeting is at the door to greet us. I tell him to go inside and fetch our brother out before he is disgraced by the teachers and before the people lynch him for being a false teacher, or worse. "Tell him his mother and brothers are outside," I say to him as he quickly disappears into the mass of bodies inside.

We wait impatiently. I don't know what's being said within amongst the crowd packed in like sardines. From what we can make out there is clearly an exchange between Jesus and the teachers of the law, but it seems that the people are not so easily swayed by the authority of the elders, who apparently have been admonished by Jesus' words.

"Furthermore," our friend relays when he returns to us outside, repeating what he'd heard Jesus say within, "'these people here', he said pointing to the crowd, 'are my family, my mother and brothers'. It didn't sound like he was that eager to come out to meet you."

I am furious and make it clear as I rant outside the house with my brothers. I can see my mother is disappointed that Jesus hasn't come out, but at the same time she seems content that Jesus is doing what Jesus always does - his own thing.

I don't think I'll ever understand my brother, nor why mum tolerates him so much. I'm sure one day he'll be the death of me.

THE JEALOUS BROTHER
(Luke 15:11-32 & Revelation 3:19-20)

The voices are echoing in my head, chasing me. I'm running, trying to hide. The damp corridors are a maze and I've no idea which way to turn. Locked doors stand before me. I turn, try another, and another. I slip, the spray of groundwater splashing forward as I skid trying to regain balance. I fail to stay upright just as I glimpse the way out of the cold dank labyrinth I've wandered into. My head crashes to the floor, meeting with the rough concrete of pavement as my eyes flick awake.

I've been dreaming, again. Always the same dream.

My surroundings haven't changed; I'm still in the alleyway, huddled beneath the overhang of a theatre backstage entrance, and squeezed behind an industrial sized wheelie bin, which I manoeuver to cover my bed from prying eyes every night. There are too many revelers in the early hours pouring out of the clubs who seek a place to empty their bladders in the dark doorways of the alley; the last thing I want is to be a victim of their idiotic stupidity - I know where that drunkenness leads to, I've been there and have worn the t-shirt with shame.

I look around in the dark, rubbing my eyes for the thousandth time, hoping my circumstances have changed - they haven't. The floor is wet from the rain. Puddles seep dangerously close to the cardboard mat I lie on. The dripping sound from the overhang onto the plastic lid of the bin is thunderous, but at least tonight the freezing rain is masking the smell of discarded food waste that usually seeps from the closed container beside me. Even the usual strong smell of urine from the top of the alley is pleasantly absent tonight.

I close my eyes and the voices return.

Go home!

You're not worthy.

They all hate you.

No one loves you!

You've got nothing here, why stay?

You're an embarrassment.

Even your friends deserted you.

I am running again. The same pointless corridors. The same feeling of loss and confusion. The same panic. The same fear that death is chasing me and I can't find a way to escape it. The voices taunt me as I run, but I know they're only in my head. Part of me knows I'm dreaming.

My eyes snap awake again, only this time I stir with the hunger in my veins.

I need a fix. I rifle through the small rucksack I use as a pillow, desperately searching every pocket. I can't find what I'm looking for. I don't have anything left. My stomach sinks and my body begins to shake at the anticipation of going without. I don't know how I'm going to make it through the night.

"Dad! Dad! Oh for Pete's sake!" I exclaim in frustration. I've been talking for at least thirty seconds but I'm pretty sure he hasn't heard a word I've said. He pretty much tuned out the minute I walked into the room.

I turn to storm out, again. This has gotten to be too familiar a routine now.

Heidi licks at my palm, tasting the remains of the treat I'd just given her. She's well fed, spoilt even. She gets to eat the scraps from the table, which these days is quite considerable as mum still makes for four.

Dad stops me before I reach the door, his interest in me sparking too late. I huff my disappointment loudly.

"Don't be like that, son."

56

"Why not?" I ask. "You spend all your free moments staring out that window at the street outside. You know the timings of every bus that passes. You watch every cab, every car. He's not going to come waltzing round the corner whistling a merry tune. He's not going to roll up in some flash sports car. If and when he comes back it's likely to be in the back of a police car or in a body bag."

I look at him. His face is distorted in both sadness and anger. He's trying not to show it but I can see his eyes welling up and I know I've gone too far. I've said too much and now I can't take it back.

I shake my head, more in disappointment at myself for hurting the old man, my crime for not caring so much for my brother showing clearly against my father's grief. But what can I do? Nothing.

I turn and walk out, hoping that maybe mum will be more interested in listening to what I want to do for my birthday.

The lights are flickering. I can't tell if it's the street lights or just the synapses in my head reacting to the giddiness that is overtaking my cravings. The shadows of the alleyway are dancing, the mist of the rain conjuring echoes of dry smoke across a teenage leg filled floor tripping to an erratic bass beat. The stereo of a passing car in the distance, too loud for the time of night, fills the void to complete the picture that is luring me back to the memory of good times. A moment later and I'm back in the club.

"It closes in an hour," shouts Dean over the din of music, "are we all coming back to yours for a party?"

I shrug my shoulders thinking, stalling. I don't really want everyone coming to mine again. They keep trashing the place and partying every night is getting expensive. My money is running out. But I don't want to disappoint my friends. I don't want to let them down. I don't want to lose them if I say no.

"Sure," I say, and immediately regret it.

Dean speeds off to spread the news. I can see him telling the girls. They look across and smile. They love a place to hang out, where they can play at being bad girls without being tracked down by overprotective parents or boyfriends.

Then I see Dean saunter over to the dealers. Officially they don't exist in the club, but everyone knows who they are and how much it costs to score. They nod with a smirk. They'll bring the hard stuff that they can't sneak into the club. Here it's only pills. Outside it's powder.

I curse under my breath, but it's ok, no one can hear me.

None of them know I'm behind on the mortgage payments. None of them know I've tapped dad for all I can get. None of them know that I'm on a final warning at work for my tardiness and erratic behaviour thanks to the lifestyle I'm leading.

I wonder why no one else is having the same problems I'm having, but then I realise that they all get to go home when they're tired, and it's not their stuff that's getting trashed, and it's not their neighbours complaining.

It will get better, I lie to myself.

The one thing I know is that I can't go home. My dad would be so angry, so appalled and ashamed of me. I've wasted everything he's given me and betrayed his trust. I don't know that I'd ever be able to face him again. Not unless I can somehow win the lottery, but what are the chances of that?

The thought of a windfall lottery win brightens the end of my dream just in time to wake me to the reality around me. My eyes flick open. I'm shivering now. It's still raining. I'm still in the alleyway. I'm still an addict, and I'm still homeless.

"No, dad doesn't want me using the house for the party. I might have to hire the function room at the pub. Dad said he'll give me some money towards it but he won't pay for the whole thing."

Heidi pads softly up to me trying to get my attention. I stroke her forehead and chin. She licks my palm aware that my spoken words are not directed at her but at the unseen voice on the other end of the phone.

"He's skint. I think he gave my brother more than he originally let on...tell me about it, you'd think he'd give me at least some of my share. I swear if I find out he gave that useless sod cash that should have gone to me there will be hell to pay." As I'm speaking I realise I'm talking rubbish, I know the money dad has put aside for me is in a trust fund in my name, but it's the extra cash I suspect he's dolled out to my brother on the side that I resent, especially as he's always being so tight fisted with me.

"I'm pretty sure Dad's in line for a big bonus soon, so I'm hoping he might be in a bit more of a generous mood by the time my birthday comes around," I say more upbeat than I'm feeling. I wonder whether I can get him to stump up for the food, or maybe the bar bill as well, but I don't dare say it aloud as I know it's unlikely.

There's a cackle of chatter on the other end about who's on the invite list. The usual names are mentioned, including some I'd be keen to avoid. I raise my objections. They're countered with the argument about the girls they'll bring with them, not to mention that one has a boyfriend who can bring some cheap gear. I don't know many suppliers, if any, drugs not being a scene I've ever been in to, but it's my birthday party and I don't want to upset my friends by being a stick in the mud. Normally I don't partake. Dad wouldn't approve. But as he won't be there maybe I'll make the exception, just this once.

The voices are still in my head as I clear the rubbish. The tramp is telling me to go home. He wants me to suck it up and go cap in hand begging for forgiveness and mercy from those I turned my back on. I rebuke him. There's no way I'd be welcomed back home.

The tramp tells me that my brother has everything he wants: the roof over his head, the meals, the car, the job, the respect of my parents. "Go home and get what he gets," the tramp says as he offers me to sup from his can of lager. I reach for it but the drug fueled mirage of a lowly friend fades and the can dissipates as my fingers try to grab at it.

Disappointed I reach down and haul the bags. Two of them are split and food is spilling out onto the floor. The boss won't be happy. The restaurant produces more rubbish than the council is prepared to clear away so the unscrupulous owner pays me a pittance cash in hand to sneak around in the early morning and move it away from their back door and put it somewhere else. They don't care where it ends up: someone's front garden, a pavement, outside another restaurant, anywhere but outside their premises. The excess rubbish attracts rats, something they already have enough of. They're in danger of being closed down for health and safety violations, which they should be, but I need them to stay open; they're the only ones who will give me a job.

I turn to carry the black sacks away, thinking that I'll return to clear up the rest before the morning rush hour starts.

"Here," says the other voice, his hand held forward with a small plastic wrap in his hand with a white powder within, "take it."

I shake my head but the look on his face is insistent. He pushes his hand further forward, almost placing it into mine. I take what's on offer, knowing it will satisfy the cravings.

"You're not going anywhere are you?" he says with a wry smile. "I have a job for you."

I think to myself about where I'd rather be. I think to myself about my imaginary friendly tramp and his warnings to go home. And I think about the dealer and his luring, his tempting me to stay and deal for him. I close my eyes to the voices in my head, but when I open them he is still there. This one is very real.

I had enough money, just, to get the bus all the way, but I didn't. I got off a few stops earlier and started walking. I thought I was having a panic attack on the bus. My heart was pounding. My palms were sweating. My throat was constricting. I was beginning to find it hard to breathe. The closer I got to home the worse it got.

Stepping off the bus into the fresh air helped, but I was suddenly worried about seeing anyone I knew, or rather, them seeing me.

It felt like it had been so long since I'd been in this neighbourhood, yet everything was so familiar. Nothing had really changed. Except me. I had changed. I was no longer the young arrogant little upstart who thought he knew how the world worked, who thought he knew best, who thought he could go off on his own and do his own thing and make a fortune and live the high life. My dad had warned me. My brother had warned me. My friends had warned me. Now I was back here with my tail between my legs knowing that I'd made a fool of myself, having squandered all the provision put aside for my future, and having hurt so many of the people I loved, and who loved me.

When I left I thought no one really cared. I had the usual arguments with my parents, minor disputes now that I think back on them, though they seemed so major at the time. I guess I just wanted my independence and to leave home and spread my wings. I was fed up of being in the shadow of my brother all the time. He was always the goody two shoes, the one who could never do a thing wrong. Maybe it was because he was the older one that dad relied on him so much.

Glad that last night's rain has stopped I walk through the streets keeping my head low, following the bus route but trying to avoid eye contact with other pedestrians. No one calls my name. No one seems to notice me.

Eventually I turn the corner to my street but my legs don't want to walk any farther. I stop on the corner and fidget for a cigarette. I don't have any so I search the floor for any discarded butts. I don't see any. There's a bin by the bus stop. I walk over to it and examine the lid. There are a few cigarette butts extinguished on the metal tray. I examine them looking for one long enough to smoke and then look around hoping there is someone I can ask for a light. The only person I see is an old school friend who is walking toward the bus stop. I quickly duck my head and turn away back to the corner of the street eager to avoid him. It's a close call as I make it to the corner and pocket my stubby.

I'm now facing the wrong way. The family home, my old house, is behind me. If I turn and peer down the road I'll be able to see it. It's late in the day so I know my dad's car will be in the driveway. My brother's will most likely be parked down the side under the car port. It's Wednesday so the gardener will probably have his van on the drive also and be tending to the front lawn. If I look closely I'll probably be able to tell if the upstairs curtains are open. I may even catch a glimpse of movement there if I time it right. But all that's behind me and I don't dare turn around. In fact I contemplate keeping on walking, to keep moving back around the corner and getting on a bus all the way back home to the alleyway I've been resting my head in of late.

I stop at the junction, hesitant. I don't know what to do. I don't know what to say. I have tried to rehearse a speech in my head, telling my dad that I'm sorry and that I'm not worthy to be welcomed home, begging him just to let me sleep on the couch for a couple of nights. I'd even eat Heidi's dog snacks if that would help me not be a burden.

I shake my head. I'm mumbling to myself. My mind is frantic. My vision blurred. I spin around in desperate confusion - and there he is, standing there.

I blink and rub my eyes, checking I'm not hallucinating, my eyes welling up as I back step. I don't get far. My dad, out of breath, his chest heaving from running, his cheeks streaked and wet with tears, grabs me before I have a chance to move away or say anything. I flinch, expecting the hard hand of discipline, but instead find myself held, embraced in a tight hold I can't wriggle free of. I breathe in the deep and familiar smell of my dad's body odour, savouring his warmth. Suddenly I am a little boy again. Suddenly I am home.

"What's going on?" I ask stepping in through the back door. I'd been washing the cars out the front. Last night's rain had left dirty water splats all over the paintwork. Mine had been overdue for a clean anyway but I decided dad's needed doing as well. The task complete I had taken Heidi out the back and filled the tub to give her a good bath. She struggled at first as I tried to rub her down, she's always resistant to begin with but then she realises she enjoys being clean and lets me take the time to pamper her as I dry her and brush her hair through.

By the time I came back in I had to make a grab for Heidi to stop her running out onto the street. Someone had left the front door open.

I stepped outside. The gardener was still there but he was paying no attention to the lawn, instead he was staring out down the street and was holding his phone to his ear talking excitedly. He pauses in mid-flow to tell me what he was apparently sharing with someone else.

"It's your brother," he says pointing down the road, "he's back."

Suddenly my heart is full of dread. I snap my head sharply in the direction the gardener is pointing and see my dad with his arm around a skinny waif that vaguely looks like my younger brother. A third figure is with them and I recognise him from school. He's on the invite list for my birthday party. The three of them are laughing and joking and I can see that they too are talking to someone on the phone.

I'm seething. My blood is boiling. Dad should be mad at him, but already I can see what is going to happen: he'll get his old room back and he'll cook him a big slap up roast, or order in a curry knowing that it's his favourite take away; I wouldn't be surprised if he even let's him take his BMW out later to go out and see his mates.

I turn around and storm inside, dragging Heidi with me, knowing that once she gets a sniff of him she'll be all over him too.

I hear the chime of my phone, a message alert. I pull it from my pocket and look at the screen. Two messages come in together, followed by a third. They all say pretty much the same thing and my heart sinks. They're from my friends congratulating me on the news of my brother's return. The news, it seems, is travelling fast. My dad has wasted no time in letting everyone know; he hasn't even brought him back into the house yet. What's worse is that the messages are all saying that they're looking forward to coming round later to see my brother - apparently dad is throwing a party at the house tonight to celebrate my brother's return.

I throw my phone at the wall in anger, Heidi ducking for cover and running to another room to be away from me.

I storm up to my room, voices echoing in my head chasing me through the house.

Why stay here!
Dad's not worthy of you. He just takes you for granted.
Dad hates you.
He doesn't love you.
You've got nothing here, why stay?
Even your friends are deserting you.

I sink to the bed and put my head in my hands, a mixture of emotions ranging between fury, sadness, and guilt. I have no right to feel this way and I know it. I hear the footsteps coming up the stairs, the familiar plod of aging feet. They're not racing with excited news like I'm expecting. He knows me. He knows my moods. He knows my likely reaction.

Curiously I turn to the doorway as I sense my father hover outside the door I'd slammed. He knocks gently, a careful measured tap telling me he wants to talk, and asking if I'll let him in.

The voices are still there. Part of me is still listening to them as I stand and move to the door and tentatively reach for the handle.

OUT OF THE DARKNESS
(Matthew 12:22-23)

There I am, minding my own business, as usual. That's how I spend most of my days, sitting around keeping to myself. When I say keeping to myself what I really mean is that I don't go very far, I stay stationary, fixed to my spot, cap in hand, silently pleading with my eyes to those who get close enough. Most people steer clear of me. Most people are used to my presence and know to ignore me. Others regularly have pity; I don't know their names, nor their faces. I keep my head down and hand raised. I think those that give are split into two camps: there are those that do it out of duty and out of proud boasting, wanting to look good and pious; the other camp (you can tell the difference) they talk with kindness and give me what I need, sometimes food, sometimes clothes, occasionally even some shelter for the night. That's all I need, to be provided with the things I can't earn for myself. Not that I'm totally incapable. I am physically able, I just can't experience things the way others can. I guess this makes me a bit of an outcast. People look down on me as rejected, diseased, cursed even. Some even go as far as to call me demon possessed.

As I say, there I am sitting around minding my own business. I had a few bits of tat scattered around my feet, things I've made with my hands that I keep in a bag I carry with me. I can make things by feel, but I don't know what they look like, nor whether they resemble the things I picture in my mind. My mind is full of imagination. My mind is my world. Sometimes people pay me for the things I make, not much, but sometimes enough to buy a meal. But the ones that grabbed me, they broke my things and forced me to leave all my possessions behind, and I never thought I'd get to see them again.

Hopefully you're getting the picture of my predicament by now, if not then I'll spell it out for you - I'm blind, I cannot see a thing. But that is only the half of it. If I could have yelled for help when I was dragged off the street then I would have, but that line of communication is lost to me also. I have no voice. I cannot speak.

Before I tell more about the ones that grabbed me let me give you a brief insight into my life. Not my background, as to where I live or my family or how I lost my sight and my voice, nothing like that, but let me give you a glimpse into the darkness of my world.

Sound is my friend. Smell is my friend. Touch is my friend. All else hates me.

My world is dark. My world is insular. My world is disconnected. I see everything with an uncertain and fearful lack of confidence as I am forced to constantly look in upon myself. No one truly cares for me. I am a burden to anyone who has ever drawn close to me, so guiltily I shun them all. I don't want to be a charity case, or one of those drains on society that pulls everyone else down, but I am what I am, and that, in the society I live in, is gutter trash.

That's where I live, in the gutters, on the outskirts, on the fringes where no one knows my name nor wants to know my name.

Sorry, I don't want you to feel sorry for me. My life isn't that bad - not anymore.

I'm used to bad smells. The street sewage runs close to where I regularly sit. I tend to sit in one location so as to stay on familiar ground where I know my surroundings, and by staying seated there is little chance of me tripping over or bumping into things. My sense of smell is heightened more than most. I can pick out spices and perfumes as they pass the town gate. I can tell who has washed recently and who hasn't. I can smell those who are ill, their bodies giving off the odour of sickness that oozes from the complaints of the human condition. I can smell the dirt of the ground and the scents carried by the wind. Even the moisture in the air carries its own familiar dampness that signals for me to take cover. I've lost count of the times people have commented on how I know when to find shelter before the rain starts to fall.

Then there is my sense of hearing. I hear the whispers, the rumours, the snide comments. I hear the animals and the wheels of the carts turning. I hear the creaking of doors, the howl of the wind, the laughter of children, and the chirp of the cricket. And too often the grumble of my own stomach.

For all the things I can do society still classes me as unemployable, as something to be feared, as something God has rejected. Therefore I can't work. I can't see. I can't write. I can't communicate in any way. I couldn't even tell you my name or how old I am. I can't identify in the same way others can, and so I am unidentifiable and without identity.

Of all the things I hear on the street, of late the word has been a buzz about one thing in particular. Beneath the wails of the Pharisees and Sadducees praying through the streets acting all holy and encouraging people to do likewise. Beneath the stamping feet of the Roman patrols that try to maintain order for the Empire. Beneath the disgruntled murmurs of the everyday hardworking family trying to make an existence in our small corner of the world. Beneath it all has been the echoing name of one man.

I know a little of religion, despite not being allowed into the temple. I know a little of politics, despite not being a taxpayer. Both spectrums have been standing to attention at the command, or rather the influence of this one man.

He has caused a stir. He is making radical claims that are upsetting some and inspiring others. He has been performing so called miracles that have confused and dumbfounded the most skeptical of his opponents.

As for my opinion, well I'd never met him, but if his claims were true, if what they said about him was true, then there was no way I was about to turn down the opportunity of crossing paths with him.

Of course my problem being that I had no way of seeking him out. It wasn't as though I could go and join the crowds following him from town to town. I couldn't chase after him on the street, not that I'd be able to pick him out from the faces in the crowd anyway. I couldn't even call out his name to get his attention.

I'd heard he was nearby, moving closer. The rumour was he was coming this way. My only hope was that he would pass by the gate where I sat and he would see me when he passed by. If I was lucky he would catch a glimpse of me and take pity.

Now I know I said I didn't want people to pity me, but this is different. This guy heals people! I maybe blind but I'm not stupid. If I could get my sight back then I wouldn't have to sit on the street begging. I would be able to get a proper job. If I had a voice I could tell people that I wasn't mad, or possessed, or hopeless. People would stop looking down on me as diseased and sinful because of my condition. People might respect me for who I am and what I can do. People might know me as more than just the blind guy who begs on the street.

If Jesus was who he said he was then I hoped he would be able to see what others can't or won't, the true me beneath the dirt and grime of my reputation. That's how I hope God sees me. I hope he looks deeper and sees the inner me, and sees the potential of who I can be.

As it happens I never got the chance to stumble across his path as he passed the gate. Either he crept in quietly or he entered town by a different route. I was gutted that I'd missed my opportunity. I wondered about trying to get someone to lead me to him, but I couldn't work out how to communicate my desire to anyone, and as it happened it was one of those days when no one seemed to want to acknowledge me anyway, and so I thought God clearly didn't care about me, that I wasn't on his priority list, that I was insignificant even to him.

Then something happened that I wasn't expecting. A mob came and collected me, manhandled me down the street. I kicked and thrashed thinking I was about to get a beating (that has happened before; I'm the dog on the street everyone thinks they can kick and be justified in doing so). I'd like to say that I landed a few good punches, but sadly it's hard to find your target when you can't see them. I must have looked like a wild animal, struggling and growling as I tried to break free of their hold.

I didn't know where they were taking me and nothing in their speech gave me a clue as to their intentions.

Eventually I was thrown to the ground and I sensed everyone move back away from me. All that was bar one man. I don't know how but I immediately knew who it was. I fell before him on my knees, head bowed and hands outstretched ahead of me pleading for his help.

The crowd went quiet, a buzz of electric anticipation hanging in the air. I could taste it, the excitement and the fear. I could almost hear their thoughts as they all watched. Suddenly I was the centre of attention. Suddenly everyone wanted to see me.

I felt the tips of his fingers touch mine and then his warm comforting hands wrap themselves around my grubby little curved fingers.

And then I saw his face. Not clearly at first, but as I lifted my head and squinted my eyes I could see his bearded features and scruffy hair slowly coming into focus. It was a beautiful sight. Colour filled my senses. Shapes and images more beautiful than I had imagined leaped out at me.

My throat was dry but I felt a bubbling of air force its way up and roll over and off my tongue as a gurgling sound parted my lips. It was barely audible, but Jesus heard it. He smiled and nodded. I spoke again, this time trying to express my thanks, wonder, and praise, but the syllables were lost amongst the gasps of astonishment from all around.

I don't know how long the stunned pause lasted, it felt like a lifetime, but eventually there was a loud and rapid-fire torrent of voices arguing over what had happened. They were trying to explain away what Jesus had done. Some claimed it a miracle, others claimed it the devil's work. In the heat of the argument I seemed to get lost in the crowd as I stood back watching the townspeople, and watching Jesus as he revealed to everyone the error in their thinking.

So here I am, sitting on the street, the blind mute guy everyone recognizes. Suddenly the world is new to me. Jesus has opened my eyes and suddenly I see opportunity and hope and wonder, things that maybe those passing me by are blind to.

BADLANDS
(Luke 10:25-37)

The year old Ford kicked back with a sudden jerk and whine, followed by a metallic twang as something seemed to buckle or snap, or both, beneath the bonnet.

Jack slammed on the brakes and shifted into neutral. He checked his mirrors; the street was deserted, the dark shadows off the sidewalks barely lit by the few street lamps not yet fallen victim to the vandalism of the neighbourhood. The engine sounded fine; purring softly in the night, its bright eyes lighting the path ahead.

He shifted into first and pulled away cautiously, frightful of being stranded in a part of town where he was sure not to be welcomed.

A rattling, and a clank, and then a crippling crunch of metal howled painfully from the car's engine. "Damn it!" he whispered to himself as he slowly manoeuvred the car to the curb and switched off the ignition.

He sat for a few moments just staring out of the windscreen at the desolate street before him. Litter in its clumps blew across the street to be battered against the walls of old disused houses whose windows were either broken or boarded up; graffiti spelling tags of juvenile delinquency. One thing was for sure: no smart cars, as in flash, expensive, not even a year old Ford dared park along these streets.

He reached for his mobile phone from within his briefcase which sat on the passenger seat. "I don't believe it!" he cringed as he read the screen display with its battery icon flashing red; just to emphasize the point an audible beep signalled its dying charge. He tried it anyway. He stepped out of the car and searched a number in the address book for the recovery company he used. He found it and pressed the 'call' button. No tone. He tried again. No tone. He pulled the phone from his ear and looked at the now blank screen.

"Damn it!" he whispered again – too afraid to speak it loud for fear of alerting anyone to his present dilemma. He looked up and down the street; the highway wasn't far – a mile, if that – there would be an emergency phone there he could use.

He reached into the car, pulled his briefcase from the passenger seat and took the keys out of the ignition. He locked the car and then, with forced intention, unwillingly began to trek, or rather creep stealthily, unnoticed through the dim streets.

He felt as though he'd been walking for ages, even though he'd only covered a few blocks. He'd spent the time scuttling along listening to his own highly polished shoes tapping against the concrete floor. Only now he was aware of a dull thud behind him, keeping time with the *tip-tap tip-tap* of his own feet. He dared not look round, but instead increased his speed to a point where he was on the verge of running. The *thud-thud* of the footfall behind him not only keeping speed with him, but now seemingly joined by a second set of heavy rubber soled shoes.

He dared to take a glance back, almost tripping as his body twisted against the grain and momentum of his legs. Behind him paced two black youths clad in dark hooded attire. He turned to face the direction he was heading, his legs having every intention of running.

"Hey white dude, where ya goin'?" hissed a voice stepping out of the shadows before him and drawing him to a halt before he could gather pace. "You're on da wrong side o' town for a man dressed money neat."

Jack held his breath in fear as he heard the other two youths stride up behind him and pull to a stop so close that he could feel their hot breath on his collar as it pierced through the cold night air.

"Let's see ya wallet n' ya watch!" ordered the hooded youth before him with a well-practised manner. Jack heard a click, and through the darkness of ethnic tint of hands could see a sparkling thin sheet of steel. As though to emphasise his authority the youth held up the knife so that it passed slowly in front of Jack's eyes.

Jack froze, fear seeping through his pores as he beheld the blade in his vision. He wanted to cooperate, wanted to give them what they demanded, but his body wouldn't respond.

Suddenly, without warning, one of the men behind him gripped his right shoulder and thrust forward with his free hand. At first he thought he'd been punched, and then again a second time, but then he saw the one in front of him lurch forward with his knife and strike him in the stomach and he realised that the pain was the same. He dropped to his knees, more through shock than pain, and was then clubbed on the back of the head so that his body fell to the ground. He wasn't sure which one kicked him in the face when he was down, the one in front he supposed, a vicious kick that tore open his nose and cheek and ripped his teeth from his exposed gums as his lip was drawn up under the rubber sole of the running shoe.

As a mixture of blood and tears filled his vision Jack could hear the three yobs laughing and yelling out their prizes as they claimed them, Jack himself only vaguely attuned to the fact that they were stripping him down in order to find his treasures, tossing him about as though he were a rag doll.

"I got da case, man," cried one.

"Watch!" yelled another.

"Wallet! Car keys!" exclaimed the one who had stood in front of him.

"Grab the rings n' his chain."

"I got 'em!"

"Hey – a cell phone!"

"Gimme that," ordered the front man as they ran off into the shadows arguing amongst themselves.

Jack lay, for the most part, unconscious, oozing thick puddles of blood through the tears in his shirt onto the paving around him so that it trickled like a slow moving lava flow into the gutter over which his legs hung.

When he came to the first time, the blackness of his sealed and swollen eyelids was blinded by the radiance of an approaching car's headlights. He forced his eyes open, having no idea how long he had been unconscious. A flickering streetlight lit him intermittently as he lay undisturbed, and even with the sparse, if not totally absent footfall, he assumed little time had passed. The car, drawing closer, slowed and then stopped in the middle of the street.

Jack raised his head, a vain effort that tore at the flesh of his cheek as the grit from the ground dirt clothed his wound. He looked in the direction of the car but was blinded by a bright light, a torch being directed from the car window. In his dazed state all he could do was blink and try to squint through the light. No one got out of the car and he wondered why – surely he was of no harm to whomever it was.

Then he heard a crackle and a hiss and the sound of a distant female voice calling a number and location, and a male voice, closer, more audible, speaking the same number in reply.

The light went out and Jack gazed in surprise and wonder at the outline of the bubble globes on the roof of the car, which, as he looked, came alive with a rotating blue light illuminating the black and white of the police car.

Jack lay down his aching head, relieved, the blue flashing shining over his torn and bloody body like calming cleansing water.

Then there was a screech of tyres and those lights were fading away down the street in a hurry to be somewhere else.

They're leaving me, Jack thought. *How can they leave me, they're policemen? Maybe they've called for an ambulance. No, I would have heard them. How can they leave me?*

His anger at being abandoned drained what little strength he still had in him. His mind hoped he was wrong, that they had called it in as they sped off elsewhere, but deep down he knew they too were afraid to get out of their car in this gang controlled neighbourhood. Cursing the cowards that wouldn't help him, he slipped once more into oblivion where he expected only death to meet him.

It was a while before his senses drew him from his slumber once more, and yet again the darkness was his only timepiece. His tongue hung from his mouth and he could taste the grimy dirt that had dried and grated upon his tongue and raked along his throat as he struggled to suck in the long muscle that protruded from his mouth. Again it was blinding car lights that had disturbed him. This time they were moving fast from far down at the other end of the street. As they neared him they slowed and Jack could hear the soft hum of the engine, and from his strangled angle could make out the low side of a red sports car, a Ferrari, its bodywork obviously curious as to the figure lying by the roadside. Jack watched with sickening amusement as the electric window lowered and a suited white male peered down at him, raised an eyebrow, then his nose, and then the window.

Jack closed his eyes as he listened to the Ferrari's wheels riding smoothly along the tarmac surface of the road away from him. He wondered what type of salary would attract such a luxury; a lawyer perhaps, one that had friends enough in both high and low places, enough to feel comfortable to drive a flash car in this neighbourhood, but with sense enough not to get out and get involved. Jack was still listening to the distant hum of money when he slipped into another world – a world of harsh, painful dreams, where to scream was an agony, and to wake was a nightmare.

Through the darkness of night, in the depths of a dream, Jack saw a light – blinding and more brilliant than any light he had ever seen. *This is it,* he thought as he slept, *I'm dying. I can see the light at the end of the tunnel. I can hear the demons beating in my head trying to stop me from reaching my goal – boom boom bang boom bang. I have to reach the light. I just have to reach…*

Jack opened his eyes. In the distance a faint headlight shone through broken glass as its twin flickered indecisively.

Boom boom bang boom bang.

The demons were getting closer. They were coming to finish him off. His body was numb. The chill of the air defeated by the warmth of his own blood, of which he had spilt too much. Yet still he could hear the demons echoing in his ears, rising up and vibrating through the ground.

BOOM BOOM BOOM BANG BOOM

The bass was accompanied by a high pitched grating of metallic synthesised sounds he couldn't distinguish through his clouded eardrums. "Too loud," he whispered coarsely, then closed his eyes as though that would somehow block out the sound.

When he opened his eyes an old rust patched car, indistinguishable in make, had pulled up alongside where he lay. The driver's door opened…

BOOM BOOM BOOM BANG BOOM BANG BOOM

…bursting louder out onto the street, causing Jack to cringe at the sound of the heavy bass of the ghetto music as it pounded painfully through his already throbbing head.

Jack closed one eye; to keep them both open was a strain. He watched as a rough looking black youth stepped out, no, rushed out, of the car and ran toward him. Fearing another attack and more abuse, Jack flinched away.

"Hey, it's okay m'man, I'll get ya outa here," spoke the man gently with a heavy burden of concern in his voice.

Jack felt himself carefully lifted from the ground, like a child having fallen asleep on a sofa and being carried by his father to the comfort of his bed. The young man carried him over to his car and opened the back door before guiding Jack in and positioning him comfortably on the back seat, then closed the door to seal him in.

Jack closed his eyes momentarily, or so he thought. When he opened them they were driving along at a steady speed through streets he didn't know. He could see street lamps chasing each other as they raced passed the window. He tried to picture the face of the driver, but the information was lost, just another gang banger who owed him no favours. He was aware that he was still pouring blood, which was now soaking onto the leather seats of the car. The car's interior, in contrast to the exterior, was well cared for and clean, its main space occupied by an expensive speaker system, which he noted had been switched off for his comfort.

"Hell, will ya look at that," murmured the black driver shaking his head. "There's ya'all beat up n' bleedin' an' da cops are on traffic duty. Don't worry pal, I'll get ya to a hospital. You'll be fine." He said this last bit with deep concern as he stared through his rear view mirror at his passenger, and for a brief moment Jack met those eyes and engraved them on his memory.

Jack looked away to the police car pulled over to the side of the street as two officers, one white, one black, spoke harshly to a white suited male stood to the side of his red Ferrari.

"Jumped a red light by the looks of it," said his driver by means of explanation.

Jack tried to nod in acknowledgement but hadn't the strength. All he could think of was red: red Ferrari, red blood, his blood, all over the sidewalk and the road, over the car seat, over the black man driving, over…

When he awoke again he was in a hospital bed, a doctor leaning over him feeling the wound on his cheek.

"Good morning," said the doctor. "Welcome back to the land of the living. You had a very close shave."

"The guy…that brought…me…" His voice was hoarse, his throat as dry as cement as he tried to ask the question.

"You mean the young man that drove you here?"

Jack nodded slowly and painfully.

"He didn't leave his name. He just rushed you in and told us to take care of you. He said if he passes by later he'll come and check on you. I don't think he was keen to stick around in case they thought he was responsible for what happened to you. He took a hell of a risk bringing you here. You're lucky it was him that found you, many wouldn't have bothered to stop in that neighbourhood."

"I…know," Jack replied.

BADLANDS
(Luke 10:25-37)

His car broke down
In a dark neighbourhood.
A pale man with money
On these streets was not good.

"Hey, white man, where ya goin'?"
Hissed a voice as he walked down the street.
"You're on the wrong side o' town
For a man dressed money neat."

"Let's see ya wallet n' watch!"
Ordered the boy from the hood.
The white man, he froze, at the sound of more feet
From behind where he stood.

A click, then a flash
As the steel passed his eyes.
Then he was stabbed in the back,
A painful surprise.

A piercing blade through his flesh,
Like only a blade would,
More than once, more than twice;
To scream – oh, if only he could.

He was knocked to the floor
And kicked viciously in the head,
Then they rummaged through his pockets
And ran off leaving him for dead.

A police car turned the corner,
Its lights beaming through the dark.
It slowed near the man, and saw,
Yet no soul dared disembark.

A call to another crime
Crackled through the air,
Relieved, the wheels screeched
As the blue lights flashed, travelling elsewhere.

The white man ate dirt
As his tongue licked the floor.
He could feel his body's heat spilling through his
fingers
As he lay at death's door.

A dazzling red sports Ferrari turned the corner
To cruise down the street.
A suited white man at the wheel,
Sitting comfortably in his seat.

He slowed to a crawl
And then wound his window right down,
Then raised his eyebrow and his nose
And sped off with a frown.

Dejected and hurt,
Lay this man about to die.
His pain now numbing his senses,
Alone, unable to cry.

A rhythmic beat of music then pounding his ears
As local wheels turned the bend.
This could only mean more trouble –
All hell to the end.

The car, it rolled up and stopped.
The driver's face as black as mud,
His eyes squinting hard
As he cast sight of the blood.

The handbrake went on
And the door swung open wide,
The interior of the car clean,
Immaculate, with pride.

The black man stood over the white man,
His eyes weeping a tear.
"It's okay m'man,
I'll get ya outa here."

The black man lifted him gently
And laid him on the back seat of his car.
The blood would stain his clothes and his seats,
But his mind was not thinking thus far.

Speedily he drove,
To breaking the law he'd confess,
For he didn't want the white man to die –
Oh, he looked such a mess.

As he rushed to the hospital,
He passed by a casual sight;
A white man in a Ferrari flagged down by the police
For failing to stop at a red light.

Inside the hospital he ran,
Scurrying back with nurses and aids.
They took the white man inside and he left,
Not knowing whether the white man's life had been
saved.

The white man, he lived,
And pondered the events which had occurred,

And the kindness of an unknown black man
Whose heart he had stirred.

Badlands the poem was written in 1993 two years before the short story. I've played very much on stereotypes, not as a racist smear against any particular group, but merely because that is exactly how the parable is written and I simply chose the most obviously recognisable scenario at the time of writing.

CPC

THUGS AT THE GATE
(Matthew 21:12-17)

The officer was quite persistent but I stuck to my guns. I know my rights, and I had no intention of telling him anything. He kept asking my name and where I lived and how I came into possession of what I was holding, but I kept looking to the muddy ground churned up by the carts, or to the stone wall of the outside of the temple, or to the crowds milling about gawping at the spectacle as the guards tried to secure what remained of the crime scene inside. They demanded my attention, but I was reluctant to give it.

Yes I'd seen what had happened, but I had no intention of putting myself forward as a witness, partly because I agreed with the action taken, and partly because I had no love for the temple guards who helped enforce the corruption inside the gates.

Now I'd queued up along with everyone else. Waited my turn. Those of us paupers who couldn't afford to spend much on the annual Passover sacrifice were first in line to try and get the best of what was on offer in the market place. I'd been there since the early hours stood in line, knowing I needed to make a bee-line for one of the many bird stalls; there was no way I had enough to buy a lamb or a goat.

When I got through I was shocked at the prices. As usual they'd gone up since last year. I checked the few coins in my pouch, mum hadn't given me enough. I went from stall to stall checking the prices and trying to haggle, but there were plenty of others stood around ready to outbid me. Distraught I walked away and stood by the side of the outer court where the market was set up at the temple,

84

figuring I would wait until the crowds died down and I could barter for a better price for a pigeon that was likely spotted and mottled and not so worthy a sacrifice. I was disappointed, but it wasn't my fault.

The birds should have been set at a discount for the poor, or free. But no, too many traders were turning a profit by taking advantage of the demand of providing a sacrifice for the festival. What made it worse is that all the temple officials and rabbi's seemed to condone it, turning a blind eye and most likely taking a cut for themselves. I get it that out of towners can't necessarily bring a healthy lamb or goat a long distance, so hiking the price a little for those that can afford it makes sense, but it's got out of hand and is unfair on the rest of us.

So there I was stood around watching the crowds, waiting for my opportunity, a young teenager being ignored and thrust aside by the masses. My mother was too sick to come herself and my little sister was forced to stay home to nurse her. Life had been hard since dad had died but I worked as hard as I could to keep us afloat.

I saw a few of my friends loitering by the steps up to the gate. I sauntered over to them to waste the time and chew the fat. We were used to congregating as a group as we killed time trying to make a quick buck on the side streets, or bullishly trying to blag our way into a public meeting or tavern where we were clearly not old enough to be permitted entry. Our little gang was fairly well known by the regular guards and temple officials, as well as by some of the Roman garrison posted on our streets. Teenage louts some people called us, but in truth we weren't that bad. None of us ever got into any real trouble as we spent most of our time trying to earn a living for our families or studying religiously the faith we were expected to learn and live out as we followed the example of the temple rulers.

So there we were stood on the steps, me with one eye on the stalls and the other on the crowds climbing up towards where we stood by the gateway. That was the first time I laid eyes on him and his entourage.

I'd heard the whispers of the traders and their patrons in the market place within the temple as they muttered conversations about a triumphal entrance of a new king of the Jews into the city, with people lining the streets and cloaks and palms spread before the man on a donkey. I didn't quite know what it was all about but I heard the whispers of voices as heads turned saying to those around them, 'that's him!'

I've seen the parades of kings and governors before; surrounded by yes men and lifted high above the heads of the crowd bolstering their pompous inflated egos, but if this was 'him' then he was different from the rest.

Now I've also seen plenty of gangs entering premises before: Pharisees with their entourage stepping through the street with an aloof air of self-importance; a Roman centurion with his soldiers fanned out behind him as he marches in to command authority over a disturbance; the scam artists and protection racketeers who saunter in with their muscle bound heavies demanding attention through fear, expecting respect but receiving distain and loathing. Even our little gang of bolshy teenagers tends to bowl through the streets with an expectation of recognition as we try to rise above our station and be known as men. There was none of this as these guys entered the temple.

At a first brief glimpse you may have thought something was amiss at this group rising the steps to the temple's outer courtyard. They swooned in from the street with the preacher I had heard of in front, and his disciples trailing behind. The preacher seemed to have a purpose as he walked; he knew where he wanted to be, but that didn't stop him from stopping to greet and talk to those who approached him. He smiled and embraced people with a calm and friendly manner. His entourage looked more nervous stood behind, as if unsure of what was about to happen. Remaining peaceable to the crowd, they kept a close eye on their master as they followed his lead.

As he climbed the steps to the gate and his disciples fanned out behind him I watched the expression on his face change. Slowly his smile faltered into a frown and then into a smoldering anger. I didn't know what the problem was but I was quick to get out of the way as what seemed like a friendly group now looked to be more of a threat to all who stood in their way. There were temple guards stood at the gate, and even they stepped aside cowardly at seeing the group approach. Not that they were aggressive or an impassible mob, but they carried with them a presence that demanded attention, mainly due to the enigmatic figure that led them, and I have to say that I couldn't take my eyes off him. Watching him was like spotting a famous rich ruler enter the city, or a famed war hero known for slaying hundreds, and keeping an eye on him knowing, or hoping something exciting is about to happen, something that you can tell your friends about afterwards.

He walked passed me and my friends, not so much ignoring us, I got the impression he was aware of us stood there, but he was focused on what was beyond the great doorway to the courtyard and the market stalls within. His face was reddening. There was a fury building, but it was controlled and tempered. And then he stepped through.

As he circled the stalls, with an exasperated expression of disgust and outrage contorting his face and his body, his followers seemed to sense the change in his behaviour and tried to steer the crowds away from him, unsure themselves as to what he was about to do. Suddenly they had become his bouncers, his personal bodyguards entrusted with the charge of an unpredictable celebrity they had no control over.

I watched fascinated, but also fearful. I could see my opportunity of getting the birds I needed beginning to slip through my hands as this man began to turn over the tables of the sellers.

Money rolled across the floor sending the merchants diving to the ground to pick up their profits. Caskets of captured birds clattered to the floor, breaking open so that there was a sudden flutter of wings as pigeons took to flight and swooned above heads as they made their mad dash for freedom. Lambs and goats tied up bleated and cowered, not knowing where to turn as their owners tried to corral them together out of harm's way.

Everybody stopped what they were doing and stood aghast. Some tried arguing with the man, but he wasn't having any of it as he ranted about them turning the temple into a den of thieves, that it was a holy place, a place of prayer, and that they were stealing from the poor and from God by forcing the people to buy sacrifices that should have been given freely to those that couldn't afford it. By setting up a market in the temple itself they were profiteering from the sacrifice that should be given to God.

I had to smile, what he said made sense. He was standing up for people like my family who struggled to bring the required offering to the temple at Passover.

The guards made a move to step in and stop him but I spotted one of the temple officials shake his head ever so subtly. Most people would have missed the gesture as they were focused on the disturbance, but I was watching everyone. The guards held off under instruction. Of course they did, the temple officials were as guilty as the traders. They took a cut of the profits in allowing the stalls to be set up. If they reacted to what the man was saying and ranting about he was likely to turn his attention on them and they would have no standing, no argument with which to debate with, for it was obvious to everyone that the temple was being abused.

The preacher stopped. He had made his point. His anger was justified. He had said what should have been said a long time ago. He alone seemed to be standing up for the heart of God and the offence caused to Him. Satisfied, he stepped back towards his companions and moved back the way he had entered, back towards me. As he walked a couple of escaped doves flew ahead of him in the direction of me and my friends. They pretty much flew into my arms and seemed content in resting with me. I quickly grabbed their feet, sure not to miss the opportunity but at the same time feeling guilty that I hadn't paid the market price for them. My friends tried to stand in front of me to cover the evidence from the watchful guards and to give me a chance to walk away with them, but before I had a chance to turn the preacher locked eyes with me.

Now I was done for, I thought, and looked to the ground quickly. When I looked up the preacher and his posse had passed by and they were sauntering back down the steps. As I turned to follow them, unsure whether that was my best escape route with the doves, the preacher turned back and smiled at me and gave a slight nod before turning away again.

I looked back to the courtyard and the market stalls, then down to the sacrifice cooing in my hands, a certainty in my heart that the price had been paid on my behalf.

As I moved away from the temple I had a real urge to know more about this preacher that had caused such a stir. I secured my purchase with some string to the feet of the doves and then, like any other curious teenager, I hung about with my mates waiting to see what would happen next.

A FATAL ERROR IN JUDGEMENT

(Matthew 26/27)

Here I sit, staring down at the ground below. It doesn't seem far, and if I jump from my perch here in the tree then the soft soil would cushion a landing - not that my feet will ever touch it. The rope is tied tight around the branch and the other end of it is in my hand in a loop ready to fasten around my neck. I have played through the scenarios in my head over and over but I can see no alternative action that I can take. Shame, guilt, fear all consume me, my every thought and feeling is screaming and boiling horror from within me at what I have done.

I don't know why I did it. I don't know how I didn't see the consequences of my actions. Somehow I was blind to the truth of what would happen as though I were not in control, as if something had taken me over, a devil scheming with evil intent.

I guess it all began a few days before Passover. It would be fair to say that my thoughts had been drifting off script before then as I was growing impatient with our Lord at not fulfilling what I expected of the Messiah in standing up against our oppressors, the Romans.

I had other frustrations also which tipped me over the edge. I often held the purse for the team, ensuring our money was safe and our finances in order so that we had enough to maintain our ministry as we travelled about. We weren't rich by any means and lived from hand to mouth, living in faith that we would have enough. Money was always tight but somehow we always seemed to have just enough to get by, but the pressure of constantly watching our dwindling funds played on my mind, especially when we were forced to pay so much in taxes to the Romans.

Don't get me wrong, I loved my job, my friends, and my Lord, I just struggled sometimes with how slow things were moving as Jesus' plan didn't match up with what I expected and what I longed for.

A couple of days before Passover, can you believe that was only a few days ago - so much has happened since. We were at the house of Simon the Leper in Bethany, not that he is a leper anymore. We were amongst friends here as this was a home we had been to often. Whilst we reclined in the company of our hosts one of the women broke open an expensive alabaster jar of perfume and anointed Jesus' head, soaking his hair as he laid back at the table. I can still remember the smell now as it wafted up and filled the room. There was a moment of still dumbfounded confusion as to what was happening as Jesus accepted this treatment from the woman of the house.

What confused us was the obvious expense and the waste of such a valuable commodity. We could have sold the perfume for a good profit which would have gone a long way to keeping us going, or better still we could have given it to those in need; we could have fed many a hungry belly with that money. But Jesus didn't seem to care about that, despite all his talk about looking after the poor. In response to our protests he waffled something about the poor always being with us and how she was doing something special for him and that he wouldn't always be around to receive such a gesture. I didn't quite get it, but then I was quite miffed at his attitude and thought he was being quite a hypocrite, so anything he said at that point probably would have gone over my head.

When we left Simon's house some of us went our separate ways; we all had our various tasks to do. I slipped off on my own and hid myself away behind a building thinking for a short while. Well, when I say I was thinking what I mean to say is I was really stewing.

The whole incident at Simon's house had me riled and I was beginning to think Jesus was leading us up the wrong path. We knew the Pharisee's wanted him arrested, and us disciples knew that letting Jesus go into Jerusalem during the Passover festival was dangerous.

I was beginning to think that if Jesus was out of the way for a short while then it would maybe give him thought to his approach and he would stop accepting the adoration of his followers and focus more on getting the people standing up to the Romans. If he was arrested by the Jewish leaders then it could provoke a stronger reaction from the people which the Romans would try to quash, if they came down too hard on the people then Jesus would be forced to speak up against them.

Such was my thinking and it didn't take much for my mind to link our famished purse into the equation. If I could offer up Jesus to the Pharisees for a fee it could all work out for the good of our whole ministry: our finances would be better off, Jesus and the people would be more prepared to revolt against our oppressors, and even the Pharisees might accept him then as the expected Messiah, and Jesus would hopefully thank me afterwards.

It was a good plan, or so I thought as I made my way to the temple courts and sought an audience with the chief priests and elders. "What are you willing to give me if I deliver him over to you?" I asked them. You should have seen the fortuitous delight in their eyes as they rubbed their hands together and raided the temple coffers, producing thirty silver coins which they handed me in a pouch with instructions to seek out a convenient occasion where they could arrest Jesus without the crowd present so as to avoid a confrontation with a rabble trying to fight the soldiers.

I left pleased with my plan and keen to tell the others and to tell Jesus how clever I was being, but an element of doubt crept into my mind that he would not be pleased, or would not understand until it had all played out, and so I kept it to myself and waited for the opportune moment.

None of it turned out the way I expected it. I expected some anger from the group and I was prepared to be yelled at. In my head I had planned to avoid everyone for a couple of days as I waited for their anger to simmer down and then go to Jesus once the rabble crowd had begun to rebel against the Romans. I was sure Jesus would see the wisdom of what I had done and would welcome being released to lead his people in a stand for freedom for the people of Israel. If it had all worked out as I'd seen it in my head then I wouldn't be here now gripping the tree trunk from this height as I place my self-fashioned noose around my neck.

Even as we went for the Passover meal last night I thought all was good with my plan. We gathered in an upper room to eat. It was a peculiar meal which began strangely with Jesus insisting on washing all our feet. As we were all eating and chatting away Jesus passed a comment about someone betraying him. Immediately we all started asking who it was. He clarified it saying it was one of us in the room at which point we all started arguing amongst ourselves and protesting that surely it wasn't one of us, and each of us trying to sidle up to him quietly to ask if he meant us - you have to understand not one of us thought we were capable of betraying Jesus - we all loved him so much.

You're probably thinking that how could I have been so short sighted or deceived as to not know it was me he was talking about, but honestly, I thought what I was doing was all for his good, to help his ministry and move it forward; I'd convinced myself that what I was planning was what he wanted. I'd even planned on when and where it would happen and was prepared to slip out from the meal to set things in motion.

Eventually all the questioning died down but, being close to Jesus, I was close enough to hear Peter and John still questioning Jesus about who would betray him. I didn't hear Jesus' whispered response but as I stretched forward to dip my bread in the bowl Jesus took it from me, dipped it in and passed it back. I was thankful, for it was quite a stretch to the bowl and I didn't want to drape my garment over the food. I nodded my thanks and then took in the looks on the faces of the two men sat either side of Jesus.

"Surely you don't mean me, Rabbi?" I asked astounded.

Jesus replied with an instruction for me to do what I had to do. This I took to mean that he was aware of my plans and approved. Without hesitation I grabbed my outer cloak and headed for the door. Now it made sense to me about his comments about a betrayer. He was warning the others about what was about to happen and was probably filling them in with the details as I left the room. Hopefully that meant that the lads wouldn't be so mad at me at what appeared as a betrayal but was actually done by his consent.

When the time came for the arrest to be made all seemed to go to plan - that was until I entered the garden.

I had been nervous from the start, mainly due to the crowd that accompanied me. I thought it would only be a couple of the elders from the temple and a few guards, but instead it turned out that a large group of supporters of the chief priests and elders came armed with clubs and swords along with the soldiers.

My plan had been to enter the garden of Gethsemene, where I knew Jesus had planned for us all to spend the night, and approach him casually without any aggravation; it would be quiet there and away from the public with only his closest disciples staying with him during the night.

I held the group back by the gate and suggested that it would be best if I entered alone. They argued that it would not be good if Jesus were able to escape and the disciples flee or turn and fight. I countered that it would be easier if they seized Jesus first to prevent the others from fighting and risking injuring their master. Most agreed to this and allowed me to enter the garden with a handful of guards, admitting that they didn't know which one Jesus was. I said I would approach them in a friendly manner (they trusted me after all and would surely know what I was planning) and would greet Jesus with a kiss so that they knew which one to arrest.

Jesus and the others saw me coming, it was hard not to with the noise and torches of the crowd behind me. They were all stood together and watching me. I walked calmly up to Jesus, the soldiers close on my shoulders. I embraced Jesus gently and kissed his cheek. "Greetings Rabbi!" I said. Jesus said something in response but I didn't really hear it for things moved quickly then. The soldiers behind me grabbed Jesus and a great deal of pushing and shoving took place as I ducked to the ground to avoid a strike from someone, James it might have been, I'm not sure. Swords were drawn and one of my friends struck off the ear of the servant of the high priest. Jesus thrust his arms out to calm the situation and ordered the swords be put away. The disciples reluctantly did as they were told but whatever words Jesus said at this point were lost to me.

I had fallen deaf as the blood rushed to my head. What had gone wrong? The lads were acting as if this were all a big surprise to them. Surely Jesus had warned them this was about to happen.

The crowd I had left at the gate had rushed forward at the first sign of trouble and so there was an angry mob on both sides with Jesus stood in the middle being held by guards. Jesus said something about this being the way it was supposed to happen and it being a fulfillment of scripture. That eased my anxiety a little but seemed to unnerve the disciples as they all fled and deserted Jesus, leaving him to his fate at being led away to be interrogated by the Sanhedrin.

As they all left I found myself alone in the garden with the darkness enveloping me. I don't think even then I knew the severity of my mistake. The darkness was consuming me, eating away at my reason, convincing myself still that what I had done was the right thing and that Jesus would be pleased with me. I sat in the darkness for a while as the sounds abated and the stars above twinkled through the clouds, the thirty silver coins weighing heavily in the pouch on my belt.

I'm not going to recount all the details of what happened the next day except to give you enough of a picture as to why I have tears streaming down my cheeks contemplating my death at my own hands.

I think I slept soundly last night in the garden on my own. When I awoke and made my way back to town there was already a great kerfuffle and emotional crowds gathering in the streets. It would appear I had missed much in the early hours: Jesus had been tried by the Sanhedrin, King Herod, and the Roman Governor Pilate; Barabbas the convicted murderer had been released, and in his place Jesus had been condemned to be executed by means of crucifixion immediately.

At first I thought this was some sick joke cooked up by the lads to wind me up after what had happened during the night, but I couldn't find them anywhere as it appeared they had all gone into hiding.

Panicked I went around asking everyone I could find what was going on. They all corroborated the same story. Jesus was condemned to die.

A tidal wave of guilt hit me, smacking me to the ground with a force that should have killed me, the world spinning above my head as the truth of what I had done sunk in. This was the intention of the Sanhedrin all along: they wanted Jesus dead. Jesus knew it. He had told us so. He had told everyone that I would betray him, and I had misunderstood his meaning.

Distraught I ran to the temple and sought out the leading priests and the elders. "I have sinned," I declared, "for I have betrayed an innocent man."

"What do we care?" they retorted. "That's your problem."

I couldn't believe it. I'd been used. Worse still, I'd allowed myself to be used. How had I ever thought it would turn out any different? I begged them to take the money back. I tried to reason with them that they had made a mistake, that I had made a mistake, that Jesus was innocent and had done nothing to deserve the death penalty. They just sniggered and said it was too late, Jesus had been tried and found guilty and would be dead by the end of the day. In anger I threw the thirty silver coins at them, they bounced noisily to the floor but still they just looked at me shaking their heads as though I was a worthless annoyance.

I ran. I fled the temple. I ran through the streets, bouncing into people and into walls.

There were people lined up in procession along the streets following an armed parade, only on closer inspection this was an execution detail. I tried to get a closer look, hoping I was wrong. I wasn't. There was Jesus, bloodied with his back torn apart by the whip, his face almost unrecognizable, his shoulders weighed down with the cross beam he was forced to carry out to his own crucifixion site outside the city.

At the site of this I let out a wild agonized cry.

I had killed my Lord.

All my hopes and dreams were shattered in that one moment. Three years of ministry were gone overnight. The hope of the Messiah overthrowing our Roman occupiers was destroyed. The devastation I had caused to all whom I knew was stark in my face; their anger to me last night in the garden would be nothing to what I would face from them now. But most of all, I had betrayed the one person who knew me best, who trusted me, and in whom I had dedicated my life to. I had nothing left to live for.

I hope now you can understand why I am here now. Jesus will die a slow agonizing death nailed to a tree. Mine thankfully will be swifter; I don't have the strength to endure what he will have to go through. As I jump from my tree I hope my neck breaks cleanly, if not then I guess I deserve no less.

This is the full version. The performance version I made slightly shorter by taking out the section at Simon's house. There is a rough video of the performance on my website and YouTube channel.

CPC

GRIEF
(John 19:25)

The journey here was arduous. Nine months pregnant, riding on the back of a donkey – it was not exactly comfortable, let me tell you. And now, as the contractions draw closer and closer together, Joseph desperately searches for a place for us to stay, a warm room, a bit of privacy. And I wonder, though I try not to, what kind of world allows a woman about to give birth no place to deliver her child? If I had known then what I know now, would I still have whispered to the angel, "Let it be unto me as you have said?"

He broke my heart that day. The remark was not meant to hurt me, I know, but rather to illustrate Jesus' love for all his followers. Still, the words stung. "Who is my mother, and who are my brothers? Whoever does the will of my Father in heaven is my brother and sister and mother." In my selfish heart a battle wages – part of me cheers his huge, ever caring heart, while the other part wants to remind him who it was exactly that delivered him in a stable, who fled to a foreign country to keep him safe, who taught him to walk and talk and play. If I had known then what I know now, would I still have whispered to the angel, "Let it be unto me as you have said?"

Over three decades ago, an old prophet at Jesus' circumcision spoke of a sword that would pierce my soul. I have often wondered at his words. When Jesus left home to begin his ministry and I felt such a constant piercing ache for his presence, I thought maybe that was what the words had meant. When I heard rumors of the danger he faced at the hands of the Romans and the religious authorities and worry pierced my soul, I thought of Simeon's sword. But those feelings seem so small compared to the debilitating grief that consumes me now. I cannot think. I cannot pray. I cannot even cry. I can only stand here watching in agony as my son – my firstborn Son! – takes his final breaths.

Scene after scene from this day of horrors flash through my mind, despite my desperate attempts to stop them. Jesus, handcuffed and tried like a criminal. Jesus, bearing a brutal flogging that tore his flesh and left him nearly dead. Jesus, a crown of the cruelest thorns pressed deep into his forehead, standing on display before a hateful crowd. Jesus, dragging a huge, rough Roman cross through the streets, making his way toward his own unthinkable death. Jesus, his hands, his feet, nailed – pierced! – to this godforsaken cross. And these hours and hours of waiting for death to come, to suffocate, to drown – just take him! Just take him! It is too much... there is too much blood...

He cries out. His body slouches on the cross, done. It is over. Over. It is dark in the middle of the day, but I do not notice because my eyes are tightly closed. The earth shakes, but I do not feel it because I have already fallen to the ground and broken into a million pieces. I am surrounded by people, by friends and strangers, but I am all alone. I do not know how long I lay on the ground wrapped in my shawl willing myself out of existence, but when I look up, I see a Roman soldier, his sword drawn, piercing the side of my dead son. I physically feel the pain in my own self, in the deepest part of me. The sword has pierced my own soul too. If I had known then – if I had known...would I have been so willing to be the mother of this child? Would I have whispered to the angel, "Let it be unto me as you have said?"

THE MOCKER
(Matthew 27:39-61)

I am ashamed. I am not a nice man. I always used to think I was a pious and righteous member of the community. I obeyed the laws - all of them, including the extra ones we teachers of the law liked to add and impose on the people to keep them on the holy path. I have always been someone who has been recognised and respected amongst the people; they know me and listen to me. I am an old man who carries a certain gravitas of authority when it comes to teaching about our faith and the requirements God expects of us in our everyday living. But I fear my words are empty. I do not live the way I should, nor the way I expect others to. I quote scripture yet have little understanding of what it all means. It took for a man to die and the world beneath my feet to be shaken, quite literally, before I would question the way I had been living and before I would wonder whether I needed to wake up from the daze of religiosity I'd been drifting in.

As old as I am I have seen many a man die, and for many years I have been expectant of the day the cold grip of death would catch up with me and bring me to my knees. I thought I would be ready for it. Ready to meet my maker. Now I'm not so sure. Now I'm uncertain of the life I've led.

For years I have come out to the place where they execute the criminals. I follow the procession, jeering and condemning the convicted with the rest of the crowd. I watch as they are hoisted up on their device of death bestowed upon us by our Roman occupiers, and I observe to ensure they receive their right and proper justice. I scrutinise the proceedings to ensure that there is no interference. I make myself seen so that the people can know that the priests and teachers of the law, such as I, condemn the activity that has led these men to their deaths. And I am not the only one. We stand around as a group, nodding and mumbling to each other, passing our own judgment as though we were the ones passing sentence. I guess in this way we give permission for the common folk around us to voice their own disgust as they throw up jibes amidst the mourning of the grieving family members.

Like I say, I am used to seeing the victims of this tortuous and barbaric form of capital punishment. I know the agonising contortions of the death throes, the tears and exhausted attempts at screams of pain as the most hardened of men beg for mercy to be let down, or for their end to be sped up to avoid the inevitable drawn out searing burning that floods through their entire being as the hours slowly tick by. All the while I watch with an almost self-gratifying smirk on my face, knowing that I will never face such an ordeal.

I know the routine of the soldiers, the checks they do to ensure the last breath has expired before they take the empty carcasses that were life filled bodies down from the cross upon which they have been nailed.

For some the pain begins before they arrive here at Golgotha, 'the place of the skull' as it is known, this gruesome theatre on a hill outside the city walls. These poor men are often whipped first and forced to carry the wooden beam through the streets whilst the people shout and spit at them. I cannot comprehend the mental anguish they must go through, being condemned, tortured, and then having to face your accusers on the route, knowing your life is about to end and that you are going to endure immense drawn out pain before you can close your eyes and face the further judgment of the Supreme God.

But as I say, this was something I used to revel in. A large part of me enjoyed the parade, because I was one that would never be condemned. I was above it all. The commoners, the sinners, were beneath me.

Or so I thought.

Yes, I was part of the group whom had condemned the rogue preacher, the one who seemed to revel in painting us religious leaders in a bad light, telling the people not to act as we do. He taught them that our words were empty and our hearts cold, or something like that. To be fair I never really stopped to listen to his message to take it in, to try and understand it, but what he said was enough to upset the establishment and so we as a group were up in arms about it and demanded action be taken against him. So yes, I was one of the ones who joined in the campaign to have him betrayed and arrested and sent for trial. I was one of the ones who rallied the crowd and paid them to petition for the murderer Barabbas to be released in order that Pilate, the Roman Governor, would be forced to execute this heretic in his place. That would teach him to blaspheme. That would teach him to go round proclaiming himself to be God, and it would send a message out to anyone else who tried to falsely claim they were fulfilling the prophesy of the Messiah.

Yes, I jeered when he was whipped and beaten. I cheered when the soldiers placed a crown of thorns on his head. I egged the crowd on when they laughed and threw things at him as he walked out of the city with the patibulum crossbeam weighing down on his shoulders. And when he hung there on his cross, I too mocked him. I laughed and told him to prove himself by getting himself down. I joked at who he thought he was: an old time prophet reborn, the Messiah, the son of God - such foolish claims. Any sane man would have denounced such notions as it was obvious that any such talk could only lead to one place. Surely this man Jesus knew that when he held insistent in his identity. And so we crucified him. I crucified him. I may not have nailed him to the cross but my words and actions and my mind-set may as well have been swinging the hammer down upon his wrists and feet.

I watched to the very end, loitering in the eerie darkness that fell upon the land, which in itself left everyone on edge. It was an unusual cloud that obliterated the sun and left a bitter chill on the hill where we stood. The three convicted men hanging must have been frozen as they had been stripped of their outer clothing.

I heard him, Jesus, begging God to forgive us, interceding for us, saying that we didn't know what we were doing. We scoffed at that too. Even at his moment of death this madman was being condescending.

I heard his claims of it being finished. About time. I was eager to be back in the city. The whole event was beginning to unnerve me. I felt uncomfortable as a great oppression swam around me. I wasn't the only one to feel it. Many fled. Many others stayed, curious. I stayed out of dutiful habit. I had to see it through. We had started this, therefore we had to see it right through to the bitter end.

I saw the last heave of his chest and the last breath escape his lips. I would have turned away quickly then, but as his head drooped to its final resting place the ground beneath my feet began to shake. The beams of the wood began to rock to the point that I was scared the crosses themselves would topple with the men still attached. Cracks opened up in the hilltop, and as I looked across to the city I could see lightning cracks splintering the stone outer walls, and rooftops beginning to crumble. It got so violent that my legs gave way as my body was flung to the side. Even the sturdy legs of the Roman soldiers struggled to stay upright. It was one of these, the centurion that was posted there, that made the link to what was happening and made me realise just how blind and foolish an old man I had been. It was his comment that made me question the way I had lived my long life and made me question all that I had witnessed and the part I had played in bringing it about.

"Surely he was the Son of God!" this pagan soldier had said. A man of no faith seeing what I was blind to. I had heard the exchange between Jesus and the other two condemned men and how Jesus seemed to imply that there was hope for one of them, the one who had accepted him for who he was.

Staring up at the dead men as I struggled to find my feet, I wondered whether it was too late for me. An old fool at the end of his days suddenly questioning whether I had got it wrong. I don't know what my contemporaries thought at that moment, most of them had drifted off by this point. If I knew them as well as I thought then I suspected they would remain to their stubborn views and blindly not link the events with the timely death outside the city. They would refuse to change their mind-set and be reluctant to bend their views, at least publicly - power and position is a hard thing to let go of.

I wondered as I walked back whether I was prepared to put my faith in this man's claims; he was dead now after all. Walking back I was conflicted. I considered all the evidence of what I had witnessed, weighing it against the idea of whether I was betraying a lifetime of religious study and achievement. I had campaigned so hard against this man, and my entire way of life was embedded in a doctrine that denounced him. It was a hard choice to make, and as I said at the beginning, I'm not a nice man.

THE GUARD'S REPORT
(Matthew 28:12-4)

I see with my eyes
Yet my eyes deny sight,
For I swear this tomb
I guarded last night.

The earth shook violently;
I stumbled, I fell.
I then ran from my post
I'm afraid I must tell.

Please, don't think me mad,
For what I saw, it was frightening.
A flash so bright,
A man as of lightning.

No wait, there was more!
He wore clothes that were calm,
As soft as the snow,
Yet still I screamed with alarm.

Then the stone to the tomb
Rolled back with such ease.
I remember no more.
I collapsed, unable to breathe.

PENTECOST
(Acts 2:1-41)

Ok, so there we are stood around together like a bunch of kids hiding in the toilets from the school bully. We'd been camped out here for a while, and to be honest the smell of Pete's B.O. was getting unbearable. We were all itching to be out in the open. I couldn't tell you how many times we'd debated stepping outside on mass, but each time someone amongst us raised a fearful doubt about what would happen if we tried to speak about our Lord without him being with us. Quite frankly we were terrified of stepping out on our own, and we clung onto Jesus' words about sending us a helper.

So there we are playing our ten thousandth game of 'eye spy with my little eye' when all of a sudden there was the sound of a violent wind. I could have blamed James or John at that point, they weren't called the sons of thunder for nothing! But it was clearly no time for joking. The noise filled the house and rattled every wooden slat and beam. The door almost broke off its hinges as though someone within was trying to kick their way out.

Then, if that wasn't freaky enough, a great jet of fire flew into the room. We could feel its heat, but it didn't seem to be burning anything. As we all watched dumbfounded the flame separated into smaller pieces and moved towards each of us, each flame resting above our heads.

Now I would have to say that maybe the initial temptation should have been to pat at the flames so that our hair didn't catch fire, but none of us did. We all knew instinctively that this flame was special. It was from God. Somehow it was God! This was the helper, the Holy Spirit Jesus had spoken about. We felt its presence as God's spirit filled each one of us. Suddenly the fear and uncertainty left us and we each began to speak in different languages as we raised our hands in praise to God.

We all stumbled out babbling like lunatics. It was a joyful noise, but everyone who saw us thought we were drunk. Then they started questioning why they could all understand us in their own native tongue, which really had them stumped as they knew us all to be Galileans who, on a normal day, all spoke the same language.

Then Peter, who's normally the gobby one, but on this occasion I'll give him the credit because I couldn't have said it as well as he did, he just stood up amongst us and addressed the crowd and told them about Jesus and the Holy Spirit. As he spoke the crowd got bigger and bigger and by the end of the day we'd baptised about three thousand new believers.

CHURCH
(Acts 2:42-47)

Yeah, I was there that day. The way Peter spoke was mind blowing. Out of the great number that was there I'd say about three thousand of us believed what we were hearing and rushed forward to be baptised.

We hung on every word of the apostles teaching and were in total awe of all they said and did. I mean the miracles they did, wow, so many to recall, but if you weren't there you probably wouldn't believe it all.

There was a great sense of community and purpose; we all seemed to be singing off the same hymn sheet. If there was anyone around us who needed anything we just clubbed together and made sure no one went without, even if that meant us selling our own things to pay for it.

Every day we met in the temple courts and in our homes, breaking bread and sharing meals together, and praising God with a real sense of joy.

And every day new people were joining us and our groups were getting bigger and bigger.

If you enjoyed reading this book then please leave a review
on my Amazon page:
https://www.amazon.co.uk/C.-P.-Clarke/e/B0034P3GHW

To read FREE short stories by C. P. Clarke go to:
www.cpclarke-author.com

Check out other books in the Point Of View series - An accessible series of short stories based on Bible passages looking at the perspectives, the motives, and emotions of the characters we read about in scripture.

31684836R00067

Printed in Poland
by Amazon Fulfillment
Poland Sp. z o.o., Wrocław